"Forget Me Not"
M/M Gay Romance

Jerry Cole

This book is intended for Adults (ages 18+) only. The contents may be offensive to some readers. It may contain graphic language, explicit sexual content, and adult situations. May contain scenes of unprotected sex. Please do not read this book if you are offended by content as mentioned above or if you are under the age of 18.

Please educate yourself on safe sex practices before making potentially life-changing decisions about sex in real life. If you're not sure where to start, see here: http://www.jerrycoleauthor.com/safe-sex-resources/.

Edition v1.00 (2019.07.18)

http://www.jerrycoleauthor.com

Special thanks to the following volunteer readers who helped with proofreading: C Mitchell, AliD, RB, JayBee, Earleen Gregg, D. Fair, Julian White, Jim Adcock and those who assisted but wished to be anonymous. Thank you so much for your support.

Chapter One

Late May

"Gram, why didn't you have them call me till now?"

Melchizedek Taylor's voice was pained as he sat holding his grandmother's hand. She was asleep...well, unconscious, really, after the surgery to repair her hip. He didn't know whether or not she could hear him, and he didn't want to wake her, so he kept his voice low. She looked so frail lying there, her deeply tanned face still managing to look pale, the hands crossed over her belly as thin as her face and her body beneath the hospital blankets.

"I'll be right here when you wake up, Gram," he promised, raising her hand to kiss the paper-thin skin that was surprisingly warm to his touch.

Somehow that warmth gave him hope. At twenty-seven, Zeke, as everyone called him because his name was such a mouthful, was used to waiting and hoping. He had lived his whole life with hope as the motivation for getting out of bed, for facing each day, for pursuing his dreams. He had been a very young babe in arms when both his parents were murdered in their sleep on the reservation where he had begun his life. His grandmother, his father's mother, had been his savior, his parent, his friend. He would never have made it this far without her, and the love that made him watch her sleep, pull the covers back over her when she twitched, and check to make sure she was still breathing as the long night wore on, was as vital to him as the air he breathed.

Sighing, he sat back, after adjusting her blankets again once the tech who had come to take her vital signs had left, and opened his backpack.

4

Pulling out two fat knitting needles stuck into a ball of vividly red yarn, he let the bag slide back to the floor, removed the needles, and continued where he had left off. He looked at his grandmother's unconscious form, feeling the usual sense of calm steal over him as he knitted. He knew she would be fine. This was Lila May Taylor...she was never not fine. No matter what life threw her way, she was always fine to anyone who asked.

The sun was just beginning to push the darkness away when he caught movement and a sound from the bed. Dropping his knitting on the chair, he leaned over and took her hand in his.

"Gram? Gram, can you hear me?"

The old lady opened her eyes and looked toward the sound of his voice. He watched as she blinked slowly and then looked earnestly up into his eyes.

"Of course, I can hear you, son. My hip's what's busted, not my ears!"

Zeke chuckled, relieved she was her sassy self. "Yes, ma'am. I was just making sure because you didn't hear me a few hours ago when I first got here."

She smiled, even as she sassed him. "Can't an old lady take a break every now and then?" Her voice was thready, but loud enough he could hear her.

Zeke leaned over and kissed her cheek. "Is that what you were trying to do when you fell over Punkin?" He grinned when she glared at him. "Coz if so, I think you've had quite enough of a break to last you the rest of your life," he teased.

She cut her eyes at him, then spoiled the effect by letting her lips curl upward in a faint smile. He could relax now. She was going to be okay, so he could leave her to the doctors and nurses for a few hours. He needed to get to work, anyway. Reaching down, he secured the knitting needles in the half-finished sweater and pushed everything back into his backpack, zipping it shut.

"I have to go, for now, Gram. But I'll be back after work, okay? Be good till I get back."

"Don't seem like I have too much choice right now, son," she quipped amusedly as he leaned in to kiss her again. "You take care."

"I will. I love you, Gram."

"I love you more," she whispered as he walked away.

Happy he kept a spare set of scrubs at the nursing home where he worked, he made his way there, showered in the staff bathroom, and clocked in with minutes to spare. He went to the nursing station to be given his orders for the day and was surprised to find it unmanned. Where was Jenny? She was never late, and she ran this floor like a drill sergeant. Turning to lean his considerable bulk against the desk to wait, he heard his name called.

"Zeke, come give me a hand, please."

Looking around to find the source of the sound, he found himself looking down the long hallway to his right. Jenny was pushing two empty wheelchairs.

"What in the world...?" He rushed over and took one from her, positioning it against the wall opposite her station. "What's going on?"

"We're getting in two newbies, if you can believe it, each one needing one of these. I didn't want to be caught without them, and the morning tech will be late."

6

She went back round to sit at her desk, waking the screen she had darkened and logging back in. "I'll have your schedule printed out for you in a flash."

She hit a few keys and turned to the printer next to her computer. In a few seconds, it spat out a sheet of paper which she handed to him. "This is the schedule for this week. You're going to get one of the newbies. Oh, and you'll need to tell me when you're taking your vacation...it'll be the end of the year soon, and you're one of only three people who hasn't taken your days yet. Remember, they don't roll over, and you won't get paid for all of them if..."

She stopped speaking and looked at him solemnly. Zeke understood all she left unsaid. They stopped accepting new residents because the facility's days were numbered unless they could find new funding to bail them out of the hole they'd been in for over a year. The next month or two would be their last, unless there was a miracle. People were worried about losing their jobs, and Zeke knew he should be as well. But he had always believed there was a higher power watching over him. He'd be fine...he had been all his life, even when things had been at their most bleak.

He smiled kindly at Jenny, who was the single mother of two young kids. He worried about her because he knew she was one who would suffer greatly if the nursing home closed its doors before she found new work.

"I remember," he said. "I'll take whatever time slot you can fit me into. You know I'm not fussy."

Jenny eyed him with a frown. "Why are you so nice?" she demanded almost angrily. "You're so damned perfect. How the hell have you managed not to be snapped up by some hot guy?"

Zeke chuckled. "First of all, I am *not* perfect! Just ask my grandmother." He grinned when she smiled at his denial. "And second of all, I'm not looking for a hot guy."

She smirked. "Tell the truth, Zeke, you're not looking for a guy at all."

"True dat!"

They laughed together before he sobered. "Don't worry, Jenny. Everything will work out. You'll see. Have faith!" He smiled and straightened up. "I'd better get a move on. You know Mrs. Z. If I'm not there on the dot of ten after, she's snippy for the rest of the day."

Jenny slanted him a rueful grin. "Have a great day, Zeke. Maybe if you're not busy, we can have lunch together."

He nodded as he walked off. He would check his duty roster after he attended to Mrs. Zupinsky. He collected a computer cart on the way and walked into Mrs. Z's room just as she reached for the TV remote to switch on the morning news.

"Good morning, Mrs. Z," he said cheerfully, signing in and pulling up the screen with her records.

"Good morning, handsome Mel," she said. Zeke chuckled. She was the only person he knew who called him Mel because, she said, "You don't look like a Zeke to me, handsome Mel."

"How are you feeling today?" he continued, getting the items he needed ready.

"Fit as a fiddle, sweetie," she replied with a mischievous smile. "And you're looking pretty fit yourself, there." She winked at him, and he laughed softly.

Mrs. Z was ninety-nine years old, but the way she flirted with him and any other man who attended to her was amusing and endearing. No one seeing how chipper she was now would ever think she could be a misery if thwarted. She liked her routines, and when they were not followed precisely, it upset her and set her off. Then no one was happy to deal with her.

"I keep telling you I'm not the guy for you," he retorted.

"I bet I could win you over to the dark side," she said with a wicked chuckle, making Zeke laugh again.

"Behave yourself, lady!" he said, pretending to be stern.

"Who says I'm misbehaving?"

Zeke shook his head with a grin. "I do. Now hush. I'm just going to check your temperature and blood pressure, okay?"

Mrs. Z reminded him of his own grandmother, and he sobered as he thought of her in the hospital recovering from surgery. She nodded as he took her temperature, checked her pulse and her blood pressure, and noted the results on her chart.

"Did you remember to make your meal orders for today last night, Mrs. Z?" he asked as he put things away and closed her chart on the computer.

"Yes, I did, thank you. I hope they have the things I ordered this time."

"I hope so too, dear," he said, patting her hand. "An aide will be here soon to help you get pretty for the day, okay? I'll be back around to give you your meds with breakfast."

"Okie dokie, handsome Mel," she said, waving at him as he walked away.

He always liked starting his day with Mrs. Z. She helped set the tone for the rest of his day, even when he had more difficult residents to deal with, like the second one on his list, a former soldier with Alzheimer's disease. His family had left him at the home when they didn't know what else to do for him, especially after he had begun to become truculent. Zeke said a silent prayer for patience as he walked into the Sergeant's room and plastered a cheerful smile on his face. The old man was wide awake and staring ahead of him fixedly. Maybe today wouldn't be so bad.

"Top of the mornin' to ya, Mr. MacKenzie."

"That's Sergeant MacKenzie to you, whippersnapper!"

And so it began. Zeke did his best to be upbeat and kind, and for a change, the old Soldier was almost calm. The new patient on his roster hadn't arrived as yet, and by the time he completed his first round, it was almost nine and time to begin the meds round. Once that was done, he took a fifteen-minute break and called the hospital to check on his grandmother. They put him through to her room.

When she picked up, he said, "Gram, it's Zeke. How are you feeling?"

"As well as a hurtin' old bird can feel, son," she answered. Her voice was still weak, and Zeke wondered if she was in pain. As though she could read

10

his mind, she added, "Now, don't you be worryin' about me. If I get too uncomfortable, I'll tell somebody."

"Have you had breakfast?" he asked next.

"I wasn't too hungry, but I had a little something so I could take my meds. Now, will you stop fussin' and get back to work?"

She tried to push impatience into her voice, but Zeke could tell she was more tired than she was letting on, and maybe in some pain. Still, she wouldn't appreciate him trying to mind her business. As she liked to tell him, the day she could no longer speak for herself was the day he could start doing so.

"All right, Gram. I'll be back after work."

The rest of his day was busy, especially once the new patient arrived. Once he was settled in, Zeke spent some time getting to know him, explaining the way things worked and trying to learn everything he could about the man. He was a short, stocky man suffering from Parkinson's disease. He seemed to be very subdued, and Zeke got very little from him. He understood how hard it had to be for a person to find himself unable to do all the things he used to take for granted. Zeke couldn't imagine being unable to knit, for example, because his hands were too shaky. He felt for people like his new charge as he could see them struggling to figure out how to respond to their new normal.

Once he changed back into his regular clothes, packing his scrubs to take home to wash, he drove back to the hospital to spend the rest of the evening with his grandmother. She was dozing when he arrived, so he pulled out his cell phone and texted their neighbor, asking her to send her teenage son over to walk Punkin, his grandmother's tan pug.

I'll pass by with his money later, and thanks, he ended the text.

By the time he put his phone away, his grandmother was waking up. He waited until she saw him before asking,

"Had a nice nap?"

She smiled wanly. "It could have been longer."

When she grimaced, he immediately reached for the call button, knowing his feisty grandmother would rather tough out the pain she was clearly feeling, but not willing to let her do it so soon after major surgery. Once the nurse arrived, checked to see the drip bag needed changing, and attended to her grandmother's immediate needs, she turned to look at Zeke with a smile.

"May I have a word, Mr. Taylor?" Zeke nodded and followed her to the door. "I'm glad you're here," she began. "Your grandmother is a tough lady, but we want her to be comfortable as well while she's here with us. We want her to leave us in the best condition before rehab. Perhaps you can impress upon her the importance of not skipping her meds? The doctor won't sign off on her discharge until he's certain she'll follow the proper pain management program while she's in rehab."

Zeke nodded. "Thanks for letting me know. I'll do my best."

Back at her bedside, he pulled his knitting from his backpack and waited until she was ready to talk to him again. He knew she'd need time for the meds to kick in, and while she waited, she watched her favorite cooking shows on the network she watched most, aside from her Hallmark channel shows. He remained silent, making good progress on the sweater, but as soon as she stirred, he looked up, dropping his knitting in his lap.

"Feeling better?" he asked. He could see her eyes were clearer, her skin less ashen.

"Yes, thank you." She smiled. "How was work?"

Zeke knew that would be the extent of their conversation about the pain, and he led where she followed in the conversation. Soon, it was dinner time, he helped her to sit up, and watched as she fed herself. He knew better than to offer her any help unless she asked for it. She ate everything on her plate, polished off the ice cream she had ordered for dessert, and kept the jello and juice for later, "After lights out, when I'm feeling peckish," she told him.

"How's my baby?" she asked in the next breath.

Zeke knew she meant her dog. He was only her baby when he was hurting or when she felt the need to protect him. Which, thank God, wasn't often these days.

"Punkin's fine, Gram. Joe's gonna walk him." The relief he saw in her eyes lifted his spirit more. He didn't want her worrying about anything except getting better. "So, what did they say?"

"I told them I wanted you to be here so we can both hear it at the same time. The doctor said he'd come back after dinner."

As though she had conjured him, a tall, elegant-looking man appeared in the doorway. "Good evening, Mrs. Taylor." He walked in and reached over to pat her hand, a warm smile on his face. Then he turned to

Zeke. "You must be her grandson. I'm Dr. Keegan." He shook Zeke's hand, his smile still firmly in place. Turning back to her, he asked, "May I?"

"I *would* prefer it if you sat down, Doctor," Gram said with a smile, and the man chuckled as he pulled over the other chair and sat down. "So, Zeke and I would like to know what's what," she added as he woke his tablet.

"We'll be keeping you here for the next six days, Mrs. Taylor," he began, consulting his notes, "and during that time, you'll continue to have visits with a physical therapist. I expect you to stick to the pain management regimen I've prescribed and not to miss any therapy sessions." He paused, looking up and asking. "How was today's session?"

"Exhausting and painful."

"I'm sorry about that, Mrs. Taylor, but as the days go on, the pain and discomfort will decrease." He looked genuinely sorry.

"How long will it take for Gram to recover, Doc?" Zeke needed to know how to plan for her care.

"That will depend on how good Mrs. Taylor is, Mr. Taylor." The doctor looked over at his grandmother, adding, "If she does everything she's told to do, and keeps her therapy and doctor's appointments, it could take as little as four months. However, I caution you both not to expect it to be that short a time. It could take up to a year for her to fully recover. Remember Mrs. Taylor's age and physical condition."

Zeke nodded, though he noticed his grandmother didn't respond. Her expression was neutral. It must be awful for her to hear the doctor's words, but he was glad he was here to hear them himself.

"You will receive a full set of instructions, when it's time for Mrs. Taylor to be discharged, regarding therapy and other medical visits." He set his tablet on his knee and looked over at Zeke. "I understand from your grandmother you are an LPN, Mr. Taylor." When Zeke nodded, he ended, "I'm glad there will be someone to ensure she follows the regimen."

"I'll see to it, Doc," Zeke said with a sharp glance at his grandmother. He'd have to find someone trustworthy who wouldn't let his Gram roll over her to be her caregiver when he wasn't home.

"Well, I need to go now. It was good to meet you, Mr. Taylor." Dr. Keegan shook his hand again and turned his smiling face back to his grandmother. "Now, you be a good grandma and do as you're told. I'll see you again tomorrow."

Gram smiled at the doctor as he walked out and then turned her sharp eyes to her grandson.

"Don't think I didn't see you ganging up on me with that fine doctor," she said. She tried for a frown, then ruined it by chuckling suddenly. "Pity he's so much older than you. He would make a lovely grandson-in-law."

Zeke rolled his eyes, laughing at his grandmother's foolishness. He was quite happy single, and he wasn't about to do anything extra to find someone, even if it would make his grandmother's heart happy. When his special someone came along, he'd know it. Time enough to do something about it then.

Chapter Two

Early July

Where was he? Thaddeus Meredith III closed his eyes, then opened them again, but nothing changed. He didn't know where he was. Blinking, he turned his head from side to side, trying to figure it out. His body hurt all over. But the pain he was most conscious of, the one that made him groan when he turned his head, made him think football players were tap dancing inside his skull. That and the persistent beeping were set to drive him crazy. Closing his eyes again, he tried to focus his mind.

What could that sound be? Why were the walls of the room he was in that dull white? Why was his head hurting so badly? He opened his eyes again at a sound from the side and turned his head gingerly to see. A woman in purple pants and a matching top approached him, a bright smile creasing her cheeks when she saw that his eyes were open.

"Ah! Lovely! You're awake at last, Mr. Meredith. Welcome back."

He frowned. Back? Back? Back from where? He was confused.

"You've been mostly out of it for three days, Mr. Meredith," she said, as though he had asked the question aloud. "Your mother will be pleased to know you're fully awake and alert at last."

Maman! The thought of his mother made tears flood his eyes, though he didn't understand why. Thaddeus Meredith III did *not* cry, ever, for any reason. He needed answers. He felt more and more discombobulated, and he didn't like the feeling. Not even a little bit.

"Where am I? What happened?" This time, he heard his voice, and he sounded like a strangled frog on its last legs.

"You were in a bit of a smash-up," the nurse said. "But don't worry, we've been taking very good care of you. You're lucky to have nothing more wrong with you than badly bruised ribs and a big bump on the head." She finished checking the bag of fluids they had been piping into his vein and set about changing it while she talked quietly. "The doctor will be in to see you as soon as he gets my page. We've been waiting for you to wake up fully for a while."

He swallowed. His throat was so dry. "May I...have something to drink?"

The nurse nodded and poured him a half cup of water from the pitcher he hadn't noticed on the table next to him.

"Sip it slowly," she instructed him, finishing what she was doing and making notes on the computer she had wheeled in ahead of her. "Are you feeling any pain?"

He nodded, then winced and whispered, "Yes."

"Next time, you must tell me as soon as I get here, okay? We don't want you to hurt more than you need to."

She lifted a tube on his arm and he looked down and watched as she injected a liquid into the port that would send the medication through his veins and into the rest of his body. Hopefully, it would ease the pounding in his head. She made another note on the laptop and smiled cheerfully as she turned away.

"The doctor will be in to see you shortly, Mr. Meredith. I hope you have a good day."

He looked around him, trying to orient himself. Why was he in a hospital? It was clear that was where he was. What had happened? He shook his head, as though he thought he could shake loose the memory of what had brought him there. Nothing stirred, and he closed his eyes, willing himself not to lose focus and not to get angry, though he could feel it building inside him. He knew he didn't like this feeling of being out of control, but until the doctor or his mother came, he didn't see how he could do anything about it.

He must have dozed again, because the next time he opened his eyes, his mother was sitting next to his chair, a worried look marring her model-perfect features. He blinked to clear his vision and spoke to her quietly.

"*Maman*?"

"Oh, *mon dieu*! Thaddeus! You frightened the life out of me!"

He had an irrational urge to laugh at the absurd comment, but he refrained. She rose and came to sit on the edge of his bed, her thin, elegant hands cupping his whiskered cheeks before she leaned in to kiss each one tenderly.

"How are you feeling, *mon chéri?*"

His mother lapsed into French when she was distressed. And when he was the cause of her concern, she called him by his full name. He knew it would have been unkind to laugh at her concern.

"What happened?" he asked without answering her question.

He assumed he'd been in an accident, though he had no memory of it. And judging by the way his body felt, it must have been a rather bad one too.

"Someone rammed you at a stop light. Don't you remember?"

Tad went to shake his head, and the pain had him hurriedly changing his mind. He used his words instead.

"No. The last thing I remember was leaving with James to the airport for the trip to Paris."

The look on his mother's face said that wasn't a good sign, but she valiantly cleared her expression and said, "Well, you did have a rather large lump on your head when they brought you in, so you're probably just confused. Don't worry about it, *mon chéri*. Another day of rest and you'll remember everything, I'm sure."

Remembering not to nod again, Tad tried for a smile instead, but his face ached as well. He reached for the plastic cup and took another sip, discreetly wiggling his toes and moving his legs to see what he could find out more about his injuries. He wasn't thinking too clearly, and his head hurt so badly he was dizzy with the pain. Moving to put the cup back hurt too much, and he was thankful when his mother relieved him of it. Her eyes were full of worry and fear, and it bothered Tad because he didn't know how to fix it.

He leaned against his pillows and closed his eyes, trying to ignore the way his whole body hurt. He wasn't accustomed to being sick. He could count on the fingers of one hand, with fingers left over, the number of times he had been incapacitated by illness in his adult life. How was he supposed to do business if he was confined to a hospital bed? The thought irritated and frustrated him, and he wanted to lash out at...who was to blame for where he found himself now?

"Did I crash the car?" he asked, still sounding like he had a lot of rusty nails lodged in his throat.

His mother seemed unable to answer. She opened her mouth, then closed it, and Tad had the impression she was trying to figure out what to say to him. Everyone knew how attached he was to his rides, and he was a collector of vintage cars. Maybe he had been in an accident with one of his beloved?

"You weren't driving one from the collection, dear." His mother's voice penetrated his thoughts.

That meant he'd been in one of the two trucks he also owned. His stomach hurt at the thought he had wrapped either of those beloved vehicles around a pole or crashed them into a wall or something equally horrendous. Which might explain why his mother was so reluctant to explain exactly what had happened to him.

"Someone rammed me, you said? It must have been something bigger than my vehicles if I hurt this much, *Maman*."

She swallowed and nodded, her distress palpable, and suddenly Tad was too tired to wonder anymore. He'd find out soon enough, he was sure. For now, he'd try to concentrate on getting well enough that he could get off the damned hospital bed and get out of there. His mother's next words seemed to echo his thinking, though they irritated him beyond their intent.

"I don't think you should be worrying about the car now, Thaddeus." His mother spoke primly,

20

formally, the way she used to do when he did something wrong as a boy. "You should be more concerned about your health. You should be grateful you're alive."

What the hell? Why would she say something like that? Of course, he was glad he was still alive. He looked at her, his eyes flashing angrily, and saw the tears she was fighting to keep from falling brimming in her eyes. His anger deflated like a popped balloon. He had really frightened her, and he shouldn't be feeling this irrational anger at her for speaking the truth, especially as he didn't have all the facts. He took a deep breath to wash away the last of his anger and spoke quietly to her.

"I'm sorry, *Maman*. You must know I am very happy to be still here with you. I'll try to relax, I promise."

She slipped a handkerchief from her pocketbook and dabbed at the corners of her eyes, then at her nose, and then looked up at him with a brave smile.

"I'm happy that you're still here too, dear."

She was back in control and none too soon as a rather small man with a large head walked in just then, introducing himself as the doctor in charge of Tad's care. He shook hands with Tad's mother, then nodded to Tad, and took a seat.

"I'm Dr. Andrews, Mr. Meredith. I'm sure you'd like to know what your prognosis is," he said, "but I believe we should begin with the usual. So, I'll just take some vitals, explain to you what has happened and what we expect will happen going forward, and then answer any questions you may have."

His tone was no-nonsense, his face expressionless. Tad nodded, thinking his bedside manner left much to be desired. Still, he wasn't there to make friends, so he watched while the doctor took his vitals, recording them on the tablet he held. Then he listened as the man gave Tad a brief summary of how he had ended up in the hospital, what treatments they had already initiated, and what they would do for the time he had remaining.

"You must understand, Mr. Meredith, that your ability to be discharged early is entirely dependent on how well you follow the instructions I've forwarded to your care team. Your loss of memory may last a few more hours, or days, or longer. The headaches should gradually pass, as should any unsteadiness on your feet when you eventually get out of bed. And though you'll most likely find yourself suffering from mood swings, those should pass as well, depending on the severity of the concussion. We'll just have to monitor you closely."

He paused here and looked closely at Tad, as though he were looking for signs of that last symptom of what he had told him earlier was a traumatic brain injury. It made the headache that had not gone away seem to sharpen, and Tad squinted and frowned.

"If you're feeling pain at any point, or if the medications do not lessen the pain, you must report it to the nurses. This is vital, Mr. Meredith." The doctor's voice was as sharp as the gaze he pierced Tad with before he continued. "We'll keep you with us for the rest of the week. You'll begin physical and occupational therapy tomorrow. Depending on how well you respond to those visits, we'll send you to rehab for another week or two before discharging you home with a health professional. Your mother and I have been talking about this, and I have agreed that if she can find a suitably qualified person to remain as

22

your live-in caregiver until you have healed completely, that will be best. Do you have any questions?"

Tad had a few, like why the doctor thought he needed his mother's intervention in his affairs, as though he were a child. He felt his ire rising again and tamped it down. Maybe this irrational and inexplicable irritability was one of the symptoms of a concussion? Maybe he should ask.

"Can you tell me what some of the other symptoms of concussion are, aside from headaches?"

The doctor eyed him speculatively before asking a question of his own. "What are you experiencing, Mr. Meredith? If you share it with me, I can probably set your mind at ease, or at least help you to understand the symptom better."

Tad sighed. He might as well get this over with. "I…" How did he explain what was bothering him? "I've been feeling really angry since I woke up. I'm not normally the hot-tempered sort."

"It's normal to feel confused and angry after a brain injury such as yours. You might find your speech becomes slurred or your vision blurs." He looked sharply at Tad again, as if waiting for confirmation of his words, then went on when Tad said nothing. "If you feel aggression sometimes and despair at other times, those are also symptoms. That is why I'm urging you to share everything that's happening to you as it happens or as soon as possible after. Perhaps keeping a journal of your experiences will also help with your long-term care."

Tad wanted to ask if he would ever regain his memory, or if he would be able to do his job. He wanted to know if he could become violent and hurt himself or others. He wondered if he would lose more of himself or his memories. But the very thought that voicing those questions would make them real kept him silent. He didn't want to be the reason anything else went wrong. And he hated that he was afraid. He had never cowered in his life, and this accident was making him squirm and fret in trepidation. He cleared his throat, determined to overcome the almost paralyzing fear that was trying to take hold of him.

"Thank you, Doctor. If I think of anything else to ask, I'll let you know."

He was done for now. He was tired, and he could feel his body slumping with bone-deep weariness. He let himself relax and slide down against the pillows as his mother asked,

"Will we get meal guidelines for him to follow, Doctor?"

"Yes, Mrs. Meredith. Everything you'll need to know to take care of your son will be included in his discharge papers."

Tad closed his eyes. If all went well, he'd be home within a couple of weeks. He'd do his best to make sure nothing got in the way of that plan. He would definitely do better when he was in his own home.

The next time he woke, he was alone, and it was dark. The light from the hallway shone eerily under the bottom of the door, and the moonlight outside the open blinds shed a ghostly light on the stark furnishings of his temporary home. He turned his head, listening to the beeping of whatever machine they had him hooked up to. His eye caught sight of the drip, caught in a swath of moonlight, as it fell from the bag down the long plastic tubing into his vein. His head was still a very present ache, but he felt clearer, calmer, a little less like a body-sized wound and a little more like a man.

He closed his eyes again, something like relief washing over him. Maybe, if he kept feeling better every time he woke up, he could leave even sooner. Another dull ache made him push the thin sheets aside and swing his leg over the side. A wave of dizziness assailed him and he lay back, panting, and his bed emitted a continuous piercing shriek.

Fuck! He reached for the call button and summoned assistance. If he didn't get out of this bed soon, he'd have an accident more immediately serious and humiliating than the one he had escaped alive from.

The door opened quietly and a man walked in. "What can I do for you, Mr. Meredith?" he asked, a tired smile on his face.

"I need the bathroom," Tad said. "Quickly, please."

The tech came to the side of the bed and checked his feet, though Tad wasn't sure why. Then he helped him to stand and walked with him to the bathroom. Standing behind him to steady him, he let Tad do his business, waited while he flushed and washed his hands, and then helped him back to bed.

"Would you like anything else, Mr. Meredith?" the tech asked quietly.

Tad shook his head, regretting it almost instantly. "I'm fine now, thank you."

After the young man closed the door quietly behind him, Tad did a more thorough inspection of himself and took stock of his injuries. He understood better why everywhere hurt, since he'd been T-boned at an intersection, and his mother's words came back to him as he wiggled his toes and tried to inhale without causing extra pain to his ribs. *You should be grateful you're alive*, she'd said. And he was. It could have been so much worse. He was amazed he had escaped with so few injuries. Amnesia aside, he would heal fast, and be back to his old self. He just had to get his memories back. He felt a kind of helpless frustration that he didn't even know what he was missing from his past. What had happened in the time he had forgotten?

He fell asleep again fretting over the answer to the question and woke when his tech came to check on him and take his vitals. Why the hell wouldn't these people just let him sleep, for fuck's sake? He pulled irritably at his bottom lip and the tech must have sensed his disquiet because he smiled gently as he put the blood pressure cuff around his bicep.

"I'll be as quick as I can, Mr. Meredith, but you don't want this to register a high reading, do you? They'll make you stay longer if it does."

Tad could tell the young man was teasing him, trying to lighten his mood, and he appreciated the gesture, but he couldn't seem to get his mind to cooperate. He bit his tongue so as not to say the sharp words that sprang to his lips, and heaved a relieved sigh when the young man finished making notations on his chart and rolled the computer cart out of his room. He closed his eyes again, trying to quiet his mind, and drifted off to sleep.

Two days after he began physical therapy, he was discharged to a rehab facility where he spent the next seven days coming to terms with the fact his memory loss was more extensive than he had

26

imagined, and that also as a result of his concussion, he had some physical deficiencies he would need to work to overcome. Like the fact he stumbled a lot when he got up that first morning to take the mandated walk down the hall and back. Or the fact that once in a while he noticed his words slurring, or he forgot what he was going to say. His concussion had been pretty severe, given these issues, and the headaches seemed to come on whenever he was feeling most stressed, frightening him more than he was willing to admit.

By the end of the seventh day, however, as he was being helped back into bed after his shower, he felt much better physically than he had the week before. And his skin tingled with the excitement of knowing he was closer to being discharged to his home, albeit into the care of a live-in nursing attendant. Another week or so in rehab and he was good to go. He couldn't contain the glee that bubbled inside him. It reminded him of how he used to feel on the night before his birthday when he was a very small boy. He'd be so keyed up about his gift that he could hardly fall asleep, and when he did, he dreamed exciting dreams about what awaited him the next day. He had not been disappointed once until he turned twelve and discovered that instead of the trip to Jamaica he had been promised, he had to attend a funeral...his grandfather's.

Tad closed his eyes, feeling tears welling up. What the hell was going on? Granddad had died thirty years ago. Why was he crying now, after all this time, and feeling as though the man he had loved as much as he loved his parents had only just died? This must be the mood swing thing the doctor had warned him about. He reached for the television remote, determined not to get lost in maudlin sentimentality, and switched it on, scrolling through the channel guides to see what he might be interested in watching. He picked Frasier because he liked its dry wit and snark of the characters and watched aimlessly for a while, his mind not really on the show.

A Budweiser commercial came on, and suddenly, instead of gently ambling Clydesdales, he saw a flash of red and heard tires screaming. His body jerked as though he'd been hit, and he blinked and looked around to see if the bed was moving. All was quiet, but his heart was racing. He saw the pickup truck veering toward him, and he cried out and held up his hands, trying to escape the crash he somehow knew was coming.

"Mr. Meredith? Mr. Meredith? Can you hear me, Mr. Meredith?"

Tad came to slowly, blinking to orient himself, then covering his eyes with his hand to block out the bright lights in the room. What the hell had happened? He swallowed and licked his lips.

"Would you like some water, Mr. Meredith?" The nurse didn't wait for him to respond, but poured water from the pitcher into a plastic cup and handed it to him. "Here, sip this," he said and waiting patiently until Tad handed him the cup. "I'm going to take your vitals again, Mr. Meredith, and then the doctor will see you. You gave us all quite a scare."

"Why?" Tad's voice sounded like rusty nails on dry wood.

"Your heart monitor went off as though you were running a marathon, sir," the nurse said. "Did you have a nightmare?"

"I...I don't think so. I think I was awake."

"Well, whatever happened, it knocked you out for a bit. The doctor will need to see what's going on. Don't worry. We'll take care of you."

The young man's soothing presence helped calm Tad, though he needed to find out what had happened to him, and what that waking dream had been about. For the first time in a week, he couldn't wait for the doctor to come around. Was he remembering, at last? The images in his head remained vivid and frightening, but he would get past them to find out the truth. He had to because he wanted his life back.

Chapter Three

Late July

It had been four weeks since Gram had been released, and six since the accident. She was still in some pain, but Zeke knew his grandmother would never admit it. He settled her into bed and went to switch off the light. He was exhausted and felt curiously relieved he would no longer have to get up at the ass crack of dawn to deal with his grandmother before going in to work. It had been a difficult decision to keep working his seven to three shift, but he preferred to be the one looking after his grandmother in the evenings and overnight. Her insurance paid for a home health aide to be with her for ten hours every day, which meant Zeke had to make sure he was home in time to relieve the woman, so he wouldn't have to pay any overtime out of pocket.

But his work schedule was grueling, and when he was called in to be given his severance package from Twilight Senior Care earlier that afternoon, he had been almost buoyant with relief. Now, he could spend time looking after his grandmother himself, making sure she got the best treatment available. He would worry about finding another job when she was back on her feet. If push came to shove, he could approach the insurance company to see if they would pay *him* to be her caregiver, since he was, after all, a licensed practical nurse.

He hadn't told her as yet he had worked his last day, and though she had insisted, when he'd told her that the nursing home was on the verge of shutting down, that he should send out his resume, he had only registered with a local agency for high-end patients. He knew they'd likely never call him because he had no experience in the swankier establishments from which those clients usually took their staff. He wanted to be there for Gram for a while before looking for work without lying to her.

Sighing heavily, he turned to walk away when his grandmother called to him quietly.

"Zeke, when are you going to tell me what's eating you, boy?"

He turned back to look at her in the darkened room. He could see the outline of her face from the night light she had asked him to put in the wall socket by her bed.

"What makes you think something's eating me?" he asked, chuckling.

She harrumphed. "I've known you since before you were born, Zeke, and raised you since your parents died. So, if you think you can hide anything from me, think again."

Zeke sighed. It wasn't in his nature to prevaricate, and he and his grandmother had long ago decided it was always better to air problems so they could be resolved quickly.

"Today was my last day," he confessed. "I got my severance package and everything."

"So, all the patients have been moved?"

"Yes. The last few went this morning. Including most of the ones on my list, which is why I had to go in today."

He watched his grandmother's face as she seemed to be weighing a question in her head. Then she asked it.

"Didn't they offer to find you a new placement?"

Zeke could see the battle lines being drawn in her head at the thought that his old employers had done him wrong. This was the part he dreaded most in the conversation. Inhaling to steady his nerve, he said, "Yeah, they did, but I refused it."

Her eyes narrowed at him, a sure sign he was about to get a tongue-lashing he might never recover from. He braced himself, fighting the grin that was trying to spread his lips. He hated when his grandmother was mad at him, but it always amused him to listen to her dressing him down like he was a two-year-old.

"Aaron Melchizedek Taylor, what did you just say? That you turned down a perfectly good job offer? What possible reason could you have for doing something so darned stupid?" She paused to take a breath before adding, "And if you tell me it has anything to do with me, I'll smack the black outta you!"

Zeke choked back the laughter that was right there in his throat waiting to burst free and said nothing, just looked at her. She had basically told him not to speak the truth, and he wasn't about to lie to her. He *had* refused because of her.

"Well?" she demanded impatiently after a few seconds of no response from him. "What do you have to say for yourself?"

If she were standing, her hands would be on her hips, and if he were still a little boy, one of them would be holding the paddle she would use to tan his backside if it were a tanning offense. Which this would have been, had he been young enough. He cleared his throat and tried to find a way to respond without

32

laughing. The situation was too funny to him, but he knew his grandmother would not see it that way.

"You said not to tell you if it had anything to do with you."

Gram's eyes narrowed even further and she struggled to sit up, shooing him away when he went to help her.

"What have I told you about putting your life on hold for me?"

Zeke thought for a moment but could think of nothing specific she had ever said on the subject. He shook his head and held out his hands, palm up in question.

"Since you've forgotten, let me say it again, and this time pay attention, dammit!"

His grandmother only ever cursed when she was beyond aggravated. So Zeke knew she was livid, and she didn't even know what all his arguments were in favor of the decision he'd made. He knew he should probably be even a little bit angry with her for trying to run his life. He was twenty-seven damned years old, for crying out loud, and he didn't need anyone to tell him how to live his life. But he could never find it in himself, even as a grown man, to be mad at the woman who had taken him in when he still barely old enough to know how to wipe his own ass, and raised him like the one son she had lost. He sat down at the foot of her bed and waited for what she had to say.

"I'm your grandmother. That means I'm old. I won't always be around to bail you out when you mess up, and to comfort you when life throws you curveballs. You need to learn how to grab on to life and enjoy the ride now, before I go." She held up a hand when he opened his mouth to argue. "And don't bother with the twaddle about me having a lot of years left in me. You don't know that, so stop trying to make me feel better by pretending you do. I'm fine with where I am in life, and if I keel over tomorrow, then it's because it's time. I'm ready to go whenever the good Lord calls."

She paused again, and even in the dim light; Zeke could see the tears tracking down her cheeks. Shit! He never liked it when his grandmother cried, and he hadn't meant to do that to her now, either. He moved to catch hold of her hand, and she squeezed his fingers before speaking again.

"I don't want you making stupid sacrifices for me, Zeke. If the reason you turned down a perfectly good job offer was so you could stay home and mind me, I'm gonna tell you right now that won't fly. Dr. Keegan told you there was a facility where I would fit in just fine and get the services I need as well as all the socializing I could possibly want. And you could come see me as often as you like without jeopardizing your future. And anyway, how are you gonna snag a good man if you don't have a job when you meet him, huh? No man worth his salt wants a no-account jobless hobo for a partner."

Zeke burst out laughing at the unexpected turn in the conversation and noted the smug smile on his grandmother's face. He knew she was only half joking, wanting to make him smile because she knew he hated to see her tears. And while he had never been and would never be a no-account hobo, he was currently jobless. But he had been a saver all his life, from the day he got his first job mowing lawns when he was thirteen. He had a bit stashed away for emergencies, though he knew he shouldn't be planning to spend his savings. Something would turn up, somehow. He had faith.

"I'll be fine, Gram, I promise. I won't make any decisions that will hurt either of us."

"You better not!" she answered sharply. "Now, come gimme some sugar and then leave me be. I need some sleep."

Zeke obeyed happily and went to his own room. The little cottage they lived in was just the right size for two people with simple needs, and though he occupied what was officially the master bedroom— "Because you need a big bed for that big body", Gram had told him—his grandmother was really the leader of their family of two. And no matter what she said, he would never abandon her, even though he knew she was right that he needed to find work.

The light on his phone was flashing. He picked it up and swiped to wake it, seeing a message notification from the agency he had applied to pop up on his screen. What the hell? What were the chances on the very night he had a conversation about jobs with his grandmother, it seemed he might be about to be offered one? He shook his head in disbelief and opened the message.

Mr. Taylor,

We have a new client who needs a live-in health attendant to work with a head trauma patient suffering from amnesia and other concussion-related effects. The job would begin almost immediately as the patient will be discharged to his home sometime tomorrow. Are you available for an interview? Please respond ASAP.

Living in was not something he was normally willing to consider, and now it was going to be even

35

more of a challenge because he was still his grandmother's primary caregiver. Should he wait to answer? Tell them no? Gram hadn't been joking when she had told him not to refuse work because of her. And even though he knew she hadn't been thinking about him living on the job site, she had also made it clear she didn't need to live with him if his job took him away. He read the message again and sighed. He'd decide what to do in the morning, after he helped his grandmother with her morning needs.

Once she was settled in her favorite armchair the next morning, Zeke cleaned up the breakfast things, tidied the kitchen and went to get his phone, which began to ring as he picked it up. Walking back into the living room he said, "Good morning. Zeke Taylor speaking."

"Good morning, Mr. Taylor, this is Irene from Health Professions Job Solutions. Did you receive the text message we sent out?"

Zeke was taken aback. They had only sent the message a few hours ago. His surprise must have been evident in his silence because the woman spoke quickly into it.

"I'm just reaching out, as the situation is rather urgent and we need a quick response. If you're not interested, that's okay."

Something about the last statement struck him as odd. "Why wouldn't I be interested? It's a job, isn't it?"

An almost imperceptible hesitation preceded her reply. "The patient has suffered a serious concussion..." Her voice trailed off, as though she didn't know what else to say without breaking HIPAA laws or something.

"When would you like me to come in for the interview?" He still wasn't sure he wanted to leave his grandmother up to the attention of strangers, but he wanted to be seen to have made the effort. This way, he wouldn't be lying to her when he tried and failed to get the job. There must be something wrong with the job they were calling him about, as he had no doubt he had been a last resort.

"Actually, the client would like you to meet with the patient at their home this afternoon. The idea is that if you suit their needs, you can begin at once."

"I'm afraid that's too short notice. I have another obligation..."

The woman cut him off. "The client seems willing to talk terms, Mr. Taylor. I'm sure if they choose you, you can discuss your situation with them then. Shall I tell them you'll be there?"

She was clearly done with the conversation and impatient to get on with the rest of her job. Zeke was aware his grandmother had been listening keenly to his side of the conversation, and he knew she would be angry all over again if he refused the interview. He sighed heavily and asked,

"What time and where?"

"One o'clock," she said. "I'll text you the address and all the information you'll need for the interview. Thank you, and good luck."

She hung up before he could reply, and his grandmother was turning to him before he had hung up on his end.

"Was that about a job?" she asked pointedly. When he murmured an affirmative, she asked, "When is the interview?"

"This afternoon at one. I'll ask Mrs. Mead if she can come over for a few hours to be with you."

"Why? How long do you expect to be gone?"

"I don't know. The interview is taking place at the patient's home."

Zeke really didn't want to tell her it was a live-in position, but knowing his grandmother, she wouldn't rest until she knew everything he did about the job.

"Remember what I said, Zeke," she cautioned him. "If we need to make some phone calls about me, let's get on that right away."

He sighed, knowing he really had little choice in the matter. Gram was not going to let him off the hook this time. They spent the next hour searching for and contacting the rehabilitation facility for senior citizens with special needs recommended by Gram's doctor, and Zeke handed over the phone when it was time to speak to someone about her staying there. She knew her medical history, her meds, and her rehab requirements, and could speak for herself. Once she hung up, she seemed satisfied with the result of the conversation.

"We have an appointment to visit the facility this evening. They give tours to prospective residents and their families at certain times of the day, ending at five-thirty each evening. Tours are no longer than half an hour, and because we're doing the dinner tour, we're invited to partake with them. That gives you more than enough time to go for your interview and come back to get me."

"What about the time in between?"

"My physical therapist will be with me for an hour today. She can help me get settled so I can get

38

my afternoon nap till you get back. Just leave a snack where I can get to it on my own."

By the time Zeke was ready to leave, he had helped his grandmother with her morning exercises, tidied the house, made her snack tray, and set out her medications. She was sitting in her favorite recliner again, the tray next to her on the side table, and she was appraising him critically.

"That's a good look on you, son," she said approvingly after she had made him turn around so she could see him from the back. "Professional without being stuffy. Now go on and break a leg."

Zeke chuckled. "I'm not auditioning for a part in a movie, Gram," he protested.

Predictably, she disagreed with him. "You most certainly are. If you play your part right, this job will be yours, and then all we'll have to do is get me settled in my new residence."

Zeke tried to read her expression to see how she really felt about them living apart, but he could see nothing but positivity in her smile. He'd have to worry about that afterward, anyway. He'd be late if he didn't leave now. He kissed his grandmother's cheeks and promised to be careful when she admonished him to drive safely, and then he was off. The drive took almost half an hour, but he was so busy preparing himself for the interview in his head that he barely noticed the time passing. Until he got to the exclusive neighborhood with the McMansions where his client lived, and then he was completely distracted.

The streets, or rather avenues, were wider here and pristine beyond anything he had ever seen. The houses were mostly invisible from the road behind high fences, either man-made or natural, and the trees lining the street were well-established and beautifully maintained. His patient lived on a dead-end road, and *his* mansion was the only one on it, located at the end, butting up against what looked like a golf course and woods. Zeke drove his old minivan through wide open iron gates at least ten feet tall and up the gently sloping driveway, rounding the corner at the circular end to see a rather large house standing majestically in the curve. He wasn't sure where to park his clearly inferior vehicle, so he drove around the circle and parked it at the side, away from the front door.

There was a brass knocker as well as a doorbell on the wide wooden front door when he walked up the shallow steps to it. He rang the bell and stepped back so he could be seen clearly by anyone looking through the peephole. Less than ten seconds later, the door was opened by a smartly-dressed older gentleman with a fully-gray head of hair and a quiet smile.

"Good afternoon, sir. Mr. Taylor, I presume?" When Zeke nodded, he continued, "Please, come in. Mrs. Meredith is expecting you."

Zeke wiped the soles of his shoes off on the welcome mat before stepping into the spacious front foyer. He followed the older man, whom he assumed was the butler, to an open door at the end of the long hallway, and waited while the man knocked discreetly before stepping in. He waited patiently while he was announced.

"Mrs. Meredith, your visitor is here, ma'am."

Zeke didn't hear a response, but he was beckoned in and he stepped past the man with a quiet smile. "Thanks," he said. The butler returned his smile before leaving, closing the door quietly behind him.

A petite woman with the most beautiful face adorned by a strained smile looked up at him from her seat behind a desk. She was simply dressed, and as she stood to greet him, he could see she was slender and almost fragile-looking. But her handshake, when he took the hand she extended to him, belied that impression. Her grip was firm and strong.

"Mr. Taylor?" she asked without preamble.

"Yes, ma'am," he replied.

"I'm Jacqueline Meredith. Please, have a seat," she invited, "and thank you for coming out at such short notice."

Zeke wasn't exactly sure how to answer that, so he just smiled as he sat in the chair she indicated and waited for her to continue. He noted that she had a faint accent, though he wasn't sure exactly where she was from. Not that it mattered. His was the only background that was important now.

"I see from your résumé that until yesterday, you were employed at the Twilight Senior Care Facility. Do you only have experience with senior citizens?"

That had to be the oddest opening interview question in history, but Zeke wasn't there to critique his potential client's interviewing skills.

"No, Mrs. Meredith. I've worked with people of all ages, including very young children." All of that was in his résumé, so he wasn't sure why she would ask him that.

"I notice you don't have much experience working with private patients," she continued, looking down at the laptop in front of her again. "Why is that?"

41

Well, then, *there* was a plain question. He wondered briefly what the woman looking at him appraisingly was expecting him to say. He wasn't going to lie, and he braced himself for a quick end to the interview after he answered.

"I prefer to work in settings like the Twilight home. I can help more people in that way than I could working for a single client."

It was no more than the truth. He wouldn't add the part that he found most people who were able to afford private nursing care were much too entitled in their behavior and he had no patience for that. He didn't know the woman sitting across from him, or the patient whom he might be hired to care for, and he was never one to make snap judgments. Their obvious wealth was not a certain indicator they would be like the others he had chosen to avoid.

"Why did you accept this interview then? Surely there are other nursing homes that could use the service of such a selfless man as yourself?"

There was a sardonic edge to her voice, to her question, and he looked up to find her eyes watching him like a hawk, sharp and unblinking, as though she didn't believe him, as though she were judging him and finding him wanting.

"I promised my grandmother I wouldn't pass up any job opportunities I was given." Might as well be honest, since he was almost certain he wasn't going to get the job.

Her eyes took on a quizzical look. "Why would you need to make such a promise?"

What the hell? Another odd-assed question. He kept his features expressionless, keeping the frown off his face as he answered her.

42

"My grandmother needs a caregiver, and I'm her only living relative."

He wasn't about to go into any further details with this woman. His private business was only important if she was going to offer him the job.

"Have you been told that this is a live-in position?" she asked sharply.

"I have," he replied immediately, "but I was assured I would be able to discuss that with you at the interview if there were issues to be addressed."

"And will your grandmother's care be an issue, Mr. Taylor?" she asked.

"Only to the degree it will determine how soon I can begin here," he said, "assuming I am offered the job."

And since he wasn't assuming he would be, he didn't care how she took his reply. So, he was rather surprised when she seemed to relax and stood up.

"Please, come with me," she said, as he stood with her. "I think it's time you met your patient."

Zeke blinked. That was it? That was the whole interview? He felt like he had been driving too fast in a race car and been sideswiped, the whiplash making his head spin. He followed the little woman out of the office and up a wide, curving staircase to the second floor of the dwelling. She walked quickly, but he had no trouble keeping up with her, and before too long they stood before an open door. She stepped in and looked around. Finding whoever she was looking for, she beckoned him in and walked forward, going out through French doors to a spacious balcony. A man sat with his back to the door, looking out over the back of the property.

"Tad, Mr. Taylor is here."

Zeke watched as the man turned his head before standing. His movements were deliberate, as though he was being careful how he moved, and Zeke took note of it as the man's eyes widened before he smiled and extended a hand.

"Good afternoon, Mr. Taylor. I'm Thaddeus Meredith. It's a pleasure to meet you. Won't you sit down?"

Chapter Four

Late July

Tad resisted the urge to wipe his hand on his sweats, but the feel on his palm of the man he was facing remained, a constant reminder of the zing he felt when they shook hands. The stranger standing before him was almost as tall as he was but rugged, built like a tank, with skin like burnished gold, like the sand in parts of the Sahara. Wide-set brown eyes looked back at him from behind black-rimmed glasses, which made his pulse kick up inexplicably. Tad took in the rest of his features...a shaved but not bald head, thick eyelashes, and a nose that had clearly been broken. He had a scar down the left side of his face, from the bottom of his ear to the corner of his mouth—*bar fight?*—and a cleft in his chin. He was conservatively dressed for an interview...dark slacks, a white button-down shirt, a matching jacket, no tie.

Tad wanted to lick him. The feeling was as unexpected as it was inappropriate. But he couldn't bring himself to care, though he did manage to drag his eyes away enough to smile at Zeke's quiet "Thank you" before he sat down again. Crossing his feet at the ankles, he tried to regain his composure, especially once he heard his visitor inhale deeply. Perhaps he wasn't the only one affected by this encounter? It would be sweet if the man standing quietly before him were gay.

"I was just about to have lunch, Mr. Taylor. Will you join me?"

"Ah...that's okay. I'm fine."

That you are! Tad smiled in response, letting his eyes roam over his would-be caregiver once again. He could get very used to having this man in his home,

45

just from the eye candy value alone. And for the first time in forever, his thoughts ran in a direction he had kept rigidly under control for twenty years. What would it be like to have a man like this in his arms, in his bed? And how would he get him there, assuming he was even interested in men? Tad was so out of practice, he was certain he would botch any attempt at making a pass, let alone anything more. And as Bailey appeared pushing a tray toward them, he thought of how incredibly inappropriate having a relationship with his nurse would be. His poor mother would cringe if she knew where his thoughts had gone.

Bailey uncovered the food and turned to him with a fond smile. "Will there be anything else, Mr. Tad?"

"No, thank you, Bailey. Enjoy your lunch."

"Thank you, sir."

Once Bailey left, Tad saw his mother, who had been watching their guest like a hawk, approach the cart. He smiled at her, and she frowned slightly before smoothing her features. He was amused, though he hid it from her. She seemed to sense his attraction to the man sitting quietly waiting, and he knew she would not approve of anything between them. But for the first time in his life, Tad didn't care. Was this a part of the whole concussion making him behave oddly? He wasn't sure; it might be, but he wasn't going to question it. He had lived most of his life denying his desires and needs, and if it took his brain being jostled about inside his skull to shake him loose from that, he was going to run with it and pray it didn't change. He just had to make sure he didn't scare his target.

"Tell me about your experience, Mr. Taylor," he said, thanking his mother when she placed the tray next to him on the side table and dipping the spoon into the steaming soup. "Why did you take up nursing?"

Those were good questions to start, he thought. They were about the work, but they would give him insight into the man, as well. It might not be kosher to try to seduce the man he was also immediately sure he was going to hire, but he did deserve to know more about him than a simple résumé could tell him. He would deal with his feelings when the time came. For now, this was still supposed to be an interview, and he could at least be professional.

"I was bullied a lot when I was younger," his guest began, the timbre of his voice making Tad shiver with awareness. "I'm of mixed heritage, and I was raised by my grandmother. For a while, we lived quite close to the reservation where my mother was born and raised. I went to a school close to where we lived for the first fifteen years of my life. Until I was attacked on the way home."

"Is that how you got that scar?" Tad's mother beat him to the question.

Zeke looked at her for a second before turning his eyes out to the golf course in front of him. Tad wished he knew why he had the inexplicable urge to comfort the man sitting beside him.

"Yes."

He didn't say anything else for a moment, and Tad wondered if he should prompt him to move on.

"I was in the hospital for a couple of weeks, and when I was discharged, I knew I wanted to do something in health care."

"Why only an LPN?" his mother asked again. Tad could almost hear her judging the man for not being more.

"My grandmother didn't have the money to send me to a four-year college to get my RN, and I wanted to start working right away so I could help her with the bills. Especially since she purchased the house we live in now and was working two jobs to pay the mortgage. I was working my yard gigs, but that money was just enough to help me pay for books and supplies for school and gear for football and basketball. And to buy her thread and yarn so we could knit and crochet."

"You...knit and crochet?" This time Tad beat his mother to the punch, his curiosity piqued.

"Champion knitter," he answered with a proud smile at Tad. "I knit sweaters and blankets for the newborns at the hospital where I volunteer in the NICU. My grandmother taught me, and we entered competitions together to get money for me to pay for the two-year college. I have an associate degree and my license as an LPN."

Suddenly, Tad wasn't interested in the qualifications or the experience. He wanted to hear more about the knitting, about his grandmother raising him, about the attack that left him scarred physically, and probably emotionally as well. But his mother jumped in again, as though she knew where Tad was going and wanted to forestall any more unnecessary forays into the man's personal life. He was, in her mind, the help, nothing more, no matter how fascinating he was.

"I don't mean to be inappropriate, Mr. Taylor," she began, before proceeding to ask an inappropriate question, "but how old are you?"

Tad caught the rise of the nurse's brows before he smoothed his expression and answered shortly,

"Twenty-seven."

Damn! He's still young. Tad swallowed the last of the soup with the spark of interest that flared in his belly at the thought. *Professional, Tad. That's what you need to be right now.* He would have to jump in again to save this interview from going completely downhill. The man's age had nothing to do with his ability to do his job. And more importantly, he was the one Tad wanted, not someone his mother deemed more suitable.

"It's very admirable of you to be proactive in your studies, Mr. Taylor," he began. "I'm sure your grandmother appreciates everything you've done to help her."

Tad saw his shoulders sag, no doubt with relief, and did a fist pump in his head. He had defused a potentially volatile situation with a kind word. His years as a JAG in the Navy had taught him you catch more flies with honey than with vinegar, and he had won many cases using that strategy.

"She's happy I'm finishing my bachelor's now, yes," he said, looking Tad directly in the eye. "It's important, too, since I want to be an occupational therapist, and you need a master's degree for that."

The longer they spoke, the deeper Tad's instantaneous infatuation with this man grew. When had he ever, in his life, met someone who instantly commanded his respect as much as this young man whom he barely knew?

"I wish you the best, then," he said and flashed a warning look at his mother. He would not have her chasing his caregiver away with her rude questions.

"Thank you, Mr. Meredith."

"Are you sure you won't have even a drink?" Tad asked, finishing the soup and reaching for the hoagie next.

His visitor hesitated, and he took the opportunity to ask another question he needed an answer to immediately.

"I'm not one for formality, Mr. Taylor, so I need to know whether or not you will object to being called by something other than your title while you're with us?"

Surprise flashed in the man's eyes, and Tad realized he hadn't as yet offered him the job. Which his immediate reply made very clear.

"Does this mean I'm being hired, Mr. Meredith?" A lifted brow accompanied the question.

Tad chuckled. "It does, indeed. So, what shall I call you?"

"My name's Aaron Melchizedek Taylor, as you know," he began, "but no one calls me Aaron. That was my father's name. And since most people have a hard time saying my middle name, everyone calls me Zeke. Well, except for a patient I had at the nursing home who called me Mel."

His voice and his smile were wistful when he stopped speaking, making Tad think the patient must have been someone he liked. Had the person died, or was he just missing him or her because he no longer worked there? Either way, Tad wanted to lighten the mood.

50

"Ah, multiple choice." He grinned when Zeke chuckled. "I'll decide eventually. So, would you like some lemonade?"

Zeke nodded this time. "Thank you."

Tad handed him a tall glass into which his mother poured some lemonade from the pitcher, and he noted the sterling silver ring that winked at him from his middle finger. It was a long, thick finger, matching the veiny hand it was part of, and Tad dragged his eyes away before his suddenly randy brain could go down paths that would make it impossible for him to hide what he was thinking.

"Can you begin today, Mr. Taylor?"

Tad eyed his mother, surprised she had given in so easily. Despite his forty-two years, he had never found it easy to win his mother over to his view of things in the past, especially when it came to his well-being. It was as if she thought he reverted to being a six-year-old when it came to making decisions about his health and safety, and about his love life. Neither of his parents had been thrilled when he had come out to them as bisexual at seventeen. The year that followed had been one of the most acutely miserable in his life. Neither of them had been angry with him exactly, but their disappointment had been palpable. And while his father had mostly avoided talking about it, eventually coming to terms with it in his own way, his mother had not relented in her attempts to make him choose girls over guys.

She still kept hoping against hope that when he fell for someone, it would be a woman. And he didn't try to change her mind. He just knew she would either accept or reject whoever he fell for, but it would make no difference to his feelings. He would no longer tolerate pushing aside his desires to please anyone else. *His* time had come.

"Gram lives with me, and I will need to get her settled into alternate housing as she's still recovering from hip surgery. I can't leave her completely alone until then."

Tad's eyes sought Zeke's face. "What happened to her?" he asked, concerned.

"She fell and broke her hip," he answered. "It's been five weeks since then, and I've been partially responsible for her care, mostly at night and in the early morning before work."

"When will you be able to move in here completely?" Tad asked.

"Gram and I have a meeting at the residential rehab facility this evening at five. I'll know more then."

Tad nodded and took another bite of his sandwich. He didn't mind a few days without Zeke being as close to him as he would be until he was completely well again. This attraction he was feeling needed to be checked, and he could do that better without the object of it under his feet for a few days. He wouldn't look a gift horse in the mouth.

After lunch, Tad's mother took Zeke on a tour of the house, starting in his suite. He tried to read Zeke's expression as they moved from Tad's bedroom and bathroom to the smaller bedroom next to it that he would be occupying, to the rest of the living quarters upstairs. He didn't seem to care the bed he would be sleeping in was too small for his big body or he would be spending a great deal of his time wherever Tad was. It didn't seem to faze him when he was told he'd be taking all his meals either with Tad or with Bailey

52

and his wife, who was their housekeeper. He didn't seem to care he'd be taking over the chauffeuring job for Tad and his free time was restricted to very specific hours during the day, rather than at night. He didn't ask any questions, although Tad couldn't imagine he had none. By the time the tour had ended, Tad was anxious to hear what was going on in Zeke's mind.

"Don't you have any questions for us, Zeke?" he asked when they were back in his mother's office.

"Just one, for now. Will I need gate codes to get on and off of the property?"

"Yes, you will," Mrs. Meredith said, "but I'd like to leave that until you're actually going to be here overnight."

She paused and looked at Tad as if she knew she was treading very close to the line. Tad swallowed and inhaled to keep himself from snapping at her. Why the hell would she try to keep the codes from the man who would be working with him for as long as he needed to get well?

"I think we can pass the codes along now, Mother." He needed her to know she had displeased him, and calling her "Mother" was as good a sign as any. "Why don't you deal with the paperwork and let me handle the codes?"

She had the good grace to blush faintly and sat down, pulling a file toward her and opening it. Tad ignored her, asking Zeke for his phone instead. He input the codes as a new note, and while he was at it, added his cell phone number. Then he sent himself a message from Zeke's phone so he could add Zeke to his contacts.

"I'd prefer it if you memorized the codes, so you can delete them," Tad told him. "I should be the only one at this point who still needs them where I can find them."

At Zeke's look, he realized they had neglected to give him a full briefing on the extent of Tad's care needs. He would have to remedy that quickly.

"I'd like it if you could come in at the time you would normally show up for work," he told Zeke, "until your grandmother is settled. Will that be okay?"

"That'll be fine," Zeke replied. "I'll be here at seven in the morning. Hopefully, we can talk more about what your principal care needs are. I just have some very general information about the job."

"I've prepared a package with the relevant notes for you to review, Mr. Taylor," Mrs. Meredith said, interrupting their conversation. "I'm sure my son will be able to answer any questions you may still have afterward."

She reached across the desk and handed him a thin folder with his name and "Caregiver's Notes" written across the front cover.

"I'll need you to sign these documents for me, in addition to whatever the agency requires you to sign. On your way back, perhaps you would be good enough to hand off the copies to them?"

"Sure thing, Mrs. Meredith."

Zeke smiled and sat down when she asked him to sign the documents she prepared. Tad grinned as Zeke started at the beginning and read everything on each page of the contract before signing, initialing, or dating anything. He could see his mother losing patience, wanting to be over with the process, but he appreciated Zeke's attention to detail. He was smart not to sign off on something he hadn't read or didn't understand.

Eventually, the business side was complete, and his mother handed over a manila envelope with the copies she had made on the machine discreetly tucked away by the window.

"Welcome to our home, Mr. Taylor," she said, walking from behind her desk, signaling that the interview was over.

Tad stepped ahead of Zeke to open the door for him and smiled as he approached. "It was a pleasure to meet you, Zeke," he said. "I'll see you in the morning."

Zeke's answering smile made his day. He walked with him to the front door, which Bailey hurried to open for him.

"Have a great rest of the day, Mr. Meredith," he said, extending his hand again.

Tad eagerly accepted the handshake, glad of another chance to touch the man whose whole vibe exuded warmth and gentleness. Would he be the same tomorrow, after he had had some time to think over the odd interview he had had to endure today? And how soon would he be able to live in? Tad was suddenly impatient and couldn't stem the feeling. Finally, after all this time, someone made him want to do more than turn away. Finally, someone mattered enough for him to make the effort to get to know him better. It didn't matter that Zeke worked for him. He had to go where his gut said.

Chapter Five

Early August

Zeke had just moved into his room at the Meredith estate and was unpacking his duffel bag when a knock sounded on his door. He called out, "Come in!" but kept on putting his t-shirts and underwear away. The man whose handshake had been as firm his mother's when they had first met, and whose touch sent sparks zinging through Zeke's body every time they had reason to touch each other, was a little taller than he was, but more slender in comparison. Dressed in a t-shirt and sweats, he was tanned and toned and had clearly been used to keeping himself in good physical shape before the accident that still caused him to move with a bit of caution, like a baby barely steady on his feet.

He had a swimmer's body, sleek and muscular beneath his clothes, and his bearing was military. His salt-and-pepper hair was short on the sides, slightly longer on top, and his blue-gray eyes were framed by black eyebrows and lashes that made them pop. He sported a thin but very well-manicured beard, and the deep dimple in his left cheek made Zeke have the uncontrollable urge to sink the tip of his tongue into it. *What the hell?*

"How can I help you, Mr. Meredith?" he asked, dragging his mind away from places it had no business going. Just because his gaydar pinged every time his boss looked at him didn't mean he should indulge in fanciful thoughts about anything between them.

"Well, for starters, how about calling me Tad?"

Zeke huffed out a breath. That right there was why he should probably have said no to this job. Such familiarity was entirely inappropriate between an employee and his employer. Especially if there was even the hint of any interest between them. And God knew there was a whole ton of interest on Zeke's part. He had tried so hard to rid himself of it, and during the ten days after he had signed the paperwork, and gotten his grandmother settled into her new home— which thankfully allowed the residents to keep their pets—he had little time to think about Tad and his feelings for him.

Things had been hectic once Gram had been settled. He had to make arrangements for someone to water the plants in his home, for the cleaner to visit twice a month now instead of once a week, and to get his teenage neighbor to sleep in one night a week, so the house would appear to be occupied when he wasn't there.

Now though, standing next to his slightly-too-small bed, unpacking his clothes, every lustful thought he ever had about being with a man rose to the surface as he scented his boss' cologne. And when Tad sat on the end of the bed, bringing him even closer to Zeke, he might have whimpered a little in his mind.

"I don't think that would be appropriate, sir," he said, avoiding looking at Tad.

He put a little more distance between them, making unnecessary trips to the dresser and back to put the clothes into drawers, pretending he wasn't flustered by Tad's presence in his room, on his bed, so close he could smell him. He was certain of one thing. Allowing any familiarity between himself and this man, no matter how innocent, would be incredibly foolish on his part. He couldn't in all good conscience stay in the job if his attraction would make it hard to do what he would need to do for Tad. Tad...*should I even be thinking of this man so familiarly?*

"Surely it's appropriate if you have my permission?" Tad's voice brought him out of his reverie.

"It would make me uncomfortable."

And make me want more than I can have. He kept that part to himself, though. His response was raw and unfiltered, and it was no more than the truth. He needed to be honest from the outset if he were to avoid making any missteps. He was being paid a lot of money to care for the man currently tempting him to forget his principles and lose himself in sensation.

"Will you join me for breakfast, then? It's too early for you to already have eaten, and I fancy your company. You need to get used to being around me twenty-four seven, anyway, now you're here for good."

That was a request he couldn't refuse. Although Tad no longer had issues with his fine motor skills, so he didn't need Zeke to help him with his meals, he was still a little unsteady on his feet, and Zeke needed to be with him in case he lost his balance. Which probably explained why he was currently occupying the space at the end of Zeke's bed, though he could have chosen to sit in the chair.

In addition, he had to monitor Tad's memories as and when—or if—they returned, be there to help him through any night terrors, and make sure he took all his medications. And he would be expected to chauffeur him around in the beginning when he was stable enough to go back to work. So, getting used to being around the man was definitely required. He put his duffel bag in the closet and turned to face Tad. He settled for a compromise in what to call him.

"Lead the way, boss," he said and hid his amusement at the wry twist of Tad's lips when he heard Zeke's name for him.

In the dining room, Zeke sat in the chair across from the one Tad sat in and inhaled deeply. He had never been attracted to anyone the way he was to this man, and he wasn't sure what to make of it. He had few experiences with men, and none of them even an ounce of the appeal Thaddeus Meredith had. The man oozed sensuality from the top of his head to the bottom of feet that Zeke knew, having seen them when he had come for the interview, were the sexiest bare feet he had ever seen anywhere on anyone. What was it about this man that was so instantly irresistible?

Gathering his wits about him, he asked, "Are you ready for your neurology appointment later?"

Tad sighed. "I had forgotten I had it." He frowned before adding, "Is that because of the brain injury or because I don't want to go so I'm blocking it?"

Once again Zeke was knocked off balance by the whole unorthodox nature of their conversations. Tad kept surprising him with how candid and open he was, a quality he shared with his very plain-spoken mother. Zeke had almost no experience with people who seemed to have few if any filters, and while with Mrs. Meredith, it bordered on rudeness, with Tad it was surprising and endearing. He wasn't too sure exactly how to respond to the question, because he was still learning what the rules were for working with his patient. He settled for an evasive reply.

"I'm not really sure, but it doesn't matter. That's why I'm here, to remind you."

The man's eyes flashed briefly, a knowing and amused look clear in their depths, but he didn't respond, merely smiling at Zeke in good humor. He helped himself, knowing Tad did not appreciate being waited on. The first time he tried to help him, on the day after his interview, when he had gone in to work and they were having lunch together, Tad had snapped at him.

"I don't need a bloody babysitter! I can serve my own plate." His English accent had been remarkably pronounced, which Zeke had found almost sexily distracting, despite the burst of anger.

Zeke knew the swing from a pleasant and accommodating mood to a snappish and rude one was par for the course until Tad's head injury was completely healed. He hoped these mood swings wouldn't be permanent, because he found he rather preferred the easygoing, gentle man Tad appeared to be otherwise. In the time since he'd begun to work with him, he hadn't lost his temper like that again with Zeke, though he had seen it in his response to his mother. Though to be fair, the woman didn't make it easy for him not to snap at her. He got that she loved her son, but she was overbearing with it, perhaps in an attempt to show him Tad had support if Zeke should screw up.

Bailey brought in a carafe of coffee and a pitcher of juice.

"Good morning, gentlemen." He put the tray with the breakfast drinks down on the table, transferring them to the center between the place settings, and picked up the empty tray again. "Mrs. Meredith asked me to convey her apologies, Mr. Tad, but she has a breakfast meeting in town. She expects to be home in time for lunch. Is there anything else I can do for either of you?

"No, thank you, Bailey. I'm fine." Zeke hurried to smile his thanks, remembering not to add "Mr." before his name.

"This is lovely, thank you, Bailey."

Tad smiled at the butler, his face lighting up with warmth. As usual, Bailey's smile in response to Tad's words was full of affection, definitely not the kind of exchange Zeke would have expected between a master and his servant. He watched the man walk away and caught Tad watching him just as closely. He remembered being torn about accepting the job if they were to offer it to him because of his attraction to his boss, and now his defenses were being further eroded by Tad's unexpected response to his butler. He could hear his grandmother's voice in his head reminding him not to judge a book by its cover.

He waited until Tad helped himself to what he wanted before taking the plate with the eggs over easy, which Bailey had been making for him since he discovered they were Zeke's favorite, and adding hash browns, a pancake, bacon, and mango slices. Tad chuckled, and he looked up curiously.

"What's funny, boss?" he asked, spreading butter over the pancake and then adding syrup.

"Well, it's not exactly funny," Tad began, stifling another chuckle. "But who eats only one pancake?"

Zeke laughed quietly. "I eat them one at a time," he said. "There's no room for more on my plate. Gram would smack me if I loaded my plate like a starving child."

He changed his voice to sound like his grandmother's when she was reprimanding him, and Tad laughed out loud.

"I'd really like to meet your grandmother," he said, sobering and adding sausages and pancakes to his plate. "Can we stop by to visit her after my appointment?"

Zeke hid his surprise. Every day Tad showed another side of his complex character, and Zeke was discovering he was everything he was showing himself to be. The head trauma and his resulting shifts in mood would make it almost impossible for him to fake anything he was feeling. How did a man as rich as this one, the leader of his family's multi-million-dollar firm, the head of their estate, manage to remain so untouched by arrogance and self-importance? How did he grow up with a woman like Mrs. Meredith and not be as stiff and unbending as she was?

Zeke supposed his having been in the military had something to do with it. But even then, he didn't seem like the hard-nosed, tough-as-nails, unfeeling bastard that so many former military men turned out to be, either. He had Googled Tad, after accepting the job, and found out quite a bit about his history. He was a top-notch former JAG and had been in the service for twenty-two years, if you count the four years in the Naval Academy. His experience in military intelligence and in the Navy courts made him a great asset in his father's firm, and when that gentleman had died, his son had taken over his position in the company that bore their name. Meredith International was a leader in the practice of international law, and the firm had its fair share of famous and notorious clients, both individual and corporate, as well as a few governments.

Zeke could tell Tad was far more than met the eye, and it bothered him to see Tad struggling to remember the things that had been stolen from him by the accident. He knew his boss was frustrated by the fact the last thing he remembered was going off on a business trip a month *before* the accident. Tad had become agitated as he had spoken of it while they were having lunch a few days earlier.

"How the hell do I forget such an important thing as me doing my job?" Tad's frustration and suppressed rage had strained his voice. "Who the hell am I if I lose even a small part of who I am? Was it that unimportant a part? Could I have managed to live happily without that time?"

"You don't know for sure it's lost."

Zeke tried to be reasonable in his response, not offering comfort which he knew was unwanted. He could well understand Tad's dismay and confusion. If he couldn't recall what he had experienced and done, had it been important? And if it hadn't been important, how much else in his life was equally so?

"It may just be delayed in returning, like a business flight," he'd continued. "It's probably better to think of it as more of a suppressed rather than a lost portion of your memories."

That suggestion had earned him a growl of disdain. Tad had opened his mouth to reply, then obviously thought the better of it, and snapped his lips shut. Zeke made note of that effort to keep his emotions contained in his daily reports, and today he would be taking those notes with him to the neurologist's office.

They ate quietly. Tad was not a fan of talking during meals unless they were at the beginning or the end of it. Once breakfast was done, Zeke began the daily routine, aware that keeping Tad to a routine would help keep him focused on what he could remember of his life before the accident, and might encourage his brain to uncover the things it still hid from him. They had begun with water exercises and moved on to actual swimming now. He normally jogged in the mornings before work, but had given it up except on weekends when Tad slept in late or when he had a bad night. Now, he accompanied Tad back to his room and went to change into his own swim trunks, returning just as Tad emerged from his suite, a towel draped around his neck and flip flops on his feet.

It had taken all he had to stop the groan from sounding the first time he had seen Tad's body in nothing but swim trunks. His body was ripped, his skin boasting a permanent light tan Zeke found himself wanting to taste. It was ridiculous the thoughts that had gone through his mind that first time. Now though, after almost two weeks of water exercises and swimming, he managed to control his reaction, both mental and physical, so he could make it through the hour-long yoga and swim session without popping a boner and having to hide his body by leaving the pool first and wrapping himself in his towel. He was grateful Tad had been banned from lifting weights or doing anything else until his balance was no longer compromised and the muscles around his ribs were fully healed.

As usual, his reaction to the sight was no different than it had been every day before, and Zeke did what he had learned would help him control his body. He looked above and to the left of Tad's head or over his right shoulder, focusing on anything other than the face of the man who was even now walking by him. Was it his imagination, or had Tad deliberately walked close enough to him so his arm brushed against Zeke's chest?

The hallway was plenty wide enough there never needed to be any physical contact between them, but he also knew he hadn't imagined the fleeting feel of body against body. Then again, why would Tad do that? The guy was filthy rich, whip-smart, and old enough to know he could do a whole lot better than the help, especially when that help didn't even have a bachelor's degree and came from the poor side of town. And even more, why would Tad want to mix things up with a half-breed anyway?

Zeke knew who he was, and though he was proud of his dual African and Native American heritage, he knew for a fact most of the people with whom he had grown up, and probably most of those in Tad's circle, would be affronted and scandalized if he were to forget himself enough to carry on with his white boss. And anyway, with his charm and good looks, Tad could have anyone in his world that he wanted, so Zeke very much doubted he would think even once about making a play for *him*. Maybe he had just been off-balance. Yeah, that was most likely what had happened. It was purely accidental. Better to err on the side of common sense and caution instead of building up false hopes.

Though yoga wasn't his thing, Zeke let Tad talk him into doing the gentle stretches with him, and he had to admit it was kind of relaxing, though the first few times he felt a little tired when he was done, which was unexpected. Now he was more comfortable with it, and as they finished up and went to rinse off before entering the pool, Tad grinned at him.

"You're a natural," he said. "You're barely breaking a sweat these days."

Zeke smiled back. "It's fine now I know what I'm doing and how to breathe and pace myself."

Stepping out from under the shower head, Tad shook himself like a dog and waited while Zeke rinsed off before saying, "How about a different challenge, then?"

Zeke eyed him curiously but didn't respond. He discovered Tad liked to challenge himself, partly to speed up his body's recovery, but no doubt also in part to see if he could jog his memory. He also sensed this was part of the man's underlying personality, and he liked it a lot.

"How about an endurance test? We'll do five laps the length of the pool to start. Let's see what you've got."

Zeke chuckled. "What I *haven't* got is years in the Navy and a pool in my backyard."

As soon as he finished speaking, he realized what he said, and felt his skin heat with embarrassment. Now Tad knew he had checked him out, gone snooping to find out more about him than they had shared. Would he be upset? It wasn't as though anything he discovered wasn't already in the public domain, but it still might seem a little bit stalkerish and intrusive. He hazarded a glance at Tad after a few seconds of what felt like an awkward silence and found a look on his face Zeke could only describe as pleased. What was *that* all about? What did he have to look so pleased about?

"Been checking up on me, huh?" Tad waggled his eyebrows, looking so far from upset that it was almost ludicrous.

"I…" How the hell was he supposed to answer that without looking like a complete fool or a jerk? Tad's quiet chuckle did nothing to make him feel better.

"It's fine. I have nothing to hide." Tad let him off the hook, moving to stand at the edge of the pool before adding. "I'm flattered, though. Thanks." The wink that accompanied those words sent a thrill through Zeke.

Then he dove off the side, and Zeke followed a second later, keeping pace with him for the first two laps, glad of something to do to keep his mind off the strange end to that conversation. By the fourth lap, he was becoming a bit more winded, and Tad seemed to be picking up the pace. He fell back halfway through the fourth lap and came in at the end of the fifth lap a good ten seconds after Tad, huffing and blowing like a buffalo after a long run, while his patient seemed hardly to be winded.

"Not bad for a landlubber," Tad said after resting for a few minutes, slapping him on the back in a friendly way. "Wanna go again?"

Zeke laughed. "Why? So you can whip me more convincingly this time?"

Tad opened his mouth as if to say something, but then seemed to change his mind and smiled instead. "Just want to keep the blood pumping. See how far I can push myself before I start to feel it. We don't have to go fast if you're not up to it, but five more laps and then you can scoot out before me, the way you always do. Makes me think you're hiding something from me, though what, I can't imagine."

Tad's eyes never left his face as he spoke, making Zeke wonder what he thought he knew. And then, just before he dove off again, he added, "Five more laps. That's an order!"

His cock jerked in his swim shorts. Yeah...somehow Tad knew exactly why he was hiding from him. Zeke sighed heavily and threw himself off the side a full half-length behind Tad. He didn't try to keep up or pass him. But he had to make sure Tad was safe. At least, that's what he told himself about why he was torturing himself doing ten laps of the pool in such quick succession. Any lie in a storm, or something like that.

By the time his body had cooled from the heat of Tad's recognition, Tad was sitting on the edge watching him come in from the last lap. He swam up, touched the wall and then dragged himself to the side and hauled himself up, tired more than he had been in a while. His cock had thankfully not gone above half-mast, and he decided to wait until Tad stood before getting up himself. He could use the extra time to bring himself back under complete control.

"I'm gonna take a nap before we have to go," Tad said.

"No problem. I'll wake you an hour before it's time to leave."

Zeke watched him rise to his feet and stride over to his towel. He got up as well, walking quickly over to his own, which he wrapped around his hips. Tad walked back up the path to the house and Zeke followed closely behind him all the way to his room, where Tad turned to say, "Thanks for the swim. It was a great workout. Haven't done that in a while."

"My pleasure." Zeke felt like an idiot, but what else could he say?

"Mine, too." Tad smiled at him and turned into his room.

Zeke's breath hitched. "Don't shower without me." Shit, that had come out wrong! "I mean…"

Tad grinned wickedly as if he were pleased that he was rattling Zeke's cage. "I know what you mean. And I won't."

Zeke's face burned, but he waited until Tad closed the door behind him before exhaling sharply. He had to get his shit together or he'd have to remove himself from the case. It had been less than two weeks and already he was tripping over his words and reading into things. He wasn't there to crush on the sexy-as-fuck older guy, he was there to help him recover fully from a brain injury. They were patient and nurse. That was all. It didn't matter that Tad was the one initiating the behavior that was setting him off. He had to exert enough control to avoid trouble. He was a grown man, not a kid. He could do this…he had no choice if he wanted to keep this job. And yeah, even though he thought it was a really bad idea to play games with his boss, he still didn't want to leave. Which was really, *really* foolish on his part.

Chapter Six

Early August

Dr. Andrews smiled and shook hands with him as Tad walked into his office. The physical exam was over, and now they would discuss the rest. He knew the questions he would be asked. Had he remembered anything else? If so, what did he remember? What about the headaches? And was he still having frequent night terrors? Any more sleepwalking? He saw Zeke look over to him with concern etched on his face. Oh, yeah...he had sort of neglected to tell his nurse that last little detail. Part of it had to do with the fact he hadn't had an episode, after the first two, before Zeke had come over a week ago. The rest was pure vanity. He didn't want Zeke's sympathy. He had only been working with Tad for a week and a half, and the attraction he felt for his younger nurse was growing by the day. What he wanted from Zeke was wholly inappropriate, and had nothing to do with his health. Unless...

"No, no sleepwalking, and no night terrors since the last one," he said. "Is that good?" Anything to take Zeke's sharp-eyed gaze off him, even for a second, so he could get a grip.

"It might be," the doctor replied with a smile. "We'll know better when you're free of them for longer than a week." He consulted the notes Zeke prepared for him and turned to him for a moment to say, "Oh, and by the way, Mr. Taylor, these notes are very thorough. I appreciate them as they give me a great deal of helpful information."

Tad watched as Zeke smiled and blushed. He found it quite endearing the big guy was so shy and self-effacing. It was one of the things he was coming to appreciate about him, coupled with his unwavering patience, even when Tad got snippy.

"I'm happy you're showing such promising signs of improvement, Mr. Meredith," the doctor said. "Keep up the workout routine and the chess lessons for Mr. Taylor." He chuckled as he spoke. "That was a brilliant idea, by the way."

Another sweet smile accompanied that compliment before the doctor continued. "Keep taking the medication for the migraines as needed, and don't overdo the swimming and yoga." He looked sternly at Tad, making him wonder if Zeke had told him about their ten-lap swim in his notes. "Your ribs won't heal any faster than they're already doing, and you may re-injure yourself. So, no more endurance tests for a bit." Yeah, he'd ratted him out, damn him! "Mr. Taylor noted you were pretty wiped out after it. I see you're almost completely steady on your feet these days, with almost no hesitation. I'm very pleased with that. Keep doing the water resistance exercises, keep resting, and don't overdo anything."

After they left the doctor's office, Tad reminded Zeke of his earlier request. "Did you ask your grandmother if we could visit her today?"

Zeke's smile lit up his face in ways that warmed Tad's heart. "I did, while you were being examined. She said that would be lovely."

"I'm looking forward to meeting her. Shall we bring her a gift? Some chocolate, maybe?"

"You don't have to..."

Tad cut off Zeke's protest. "I most certainly do have to. One doesn't go visiting empty-handed if one can avoid it."

He stepped away, heading toward the chocolate shop conveniently located in the plaza where his neurologist's office was located. He walked around, wondering what Zeke's grandmother liked, when it occurred to him she might not like chocolate. Damn!

"Does your grandmother like chocolates?" He turned to find Zeke watching him with a bemused expression on his face.

"Yes. She's partial to Cadbury's milk chocolate."

Relief swept through Tad. He wanted Zeke's grandmother to like him, though he couldn't say why. He found a mini gift basket of Cadbury chocolate samples and picked it up.

"This ought to hit the spot without getting her into trouble with her doctor."

Zeke laughed, and once they were back in the car, he turned to Tad. "Gram is in better shape than most people her age. Her blood pressure and her blood sugar are normal and according to her doctor, she could use a few more pounds."

"Then I'm glad I went with my gut."

Tad smiled widely, feeling even better about his gift, if that were possible. He couldn't wait to meet the woman who had raised Zeke. He would bet good money everything he was coming to admire about the man he had learned from his grandmother. Which meant Tad would forever be in her debt...if he and Zeke ever made it past nurse and patient.

When they got to the facility, Tad felt a little light-headed with anticipation. He couldn't remember the last time he wanted something as badly as he wanted to meet Mrs. Taylor. He dutifully allowed Zeke to open his door for him, and enjoyed the feel of his hand at the small of his back as they walked in together. It was almost as though Zeke knew what was happening in his head and was giving him all the support he would accept.

"Good afternoon. I'm here to see Lila May Taylor. I'm…"

The woman to whom Zeke addressed his remarks interrupted him, smiling widely, her eyes full of an appreciation Tad could well understand. If only he knew for sure whether or not she was barking up the wrong tree. He watched Zeke closely, looking for any recognition in his response to her. He saw none, but that didn't mean Zeke would appreciate being hit on by a man, either. Still, he hadn't reacted badly to any of Tad's attempts to feel him out. Maybe he could up his game, and a visit to his grandmother might help him figure out how to do that.

"I know who you are, Mr. Taylor," the woman said. "Mrs. T speaks about you all the time. No one in the world to her like her Zeke."

Her smile was indulgent as well as interested, and Tad could understand why she might want to get to know Zeke better. He was in the same boat, but he had the advantage Zeke lived in his house. He shook his head internally at himself at how smug that made him feel.

"She's waiting for you and your guest." She turned her eyes to Tad's face then and he smiled at her, making her eyes widen. "Please, follow me."

She sounded breathless, and he grinned, pleased he had apparently not lost his appeal to women. At least he remembered being sought after by them. That memory had not been erased. The thought

74

dimmed his elation, but he pushed it away, unwilling to let anything spoil this meeting.

She spoke quietly to the other occupant of the reception cubicle before moving ahead of the two of them. He walked ahead of Zeke, who waited for him to do so, wishing he could be the one in back so he could look his fill at Zeke without having to pretend he wasn't ogling him. They walked along a long corridor, turned once, then again, and ended up in a large, airy room abuzz with conversation. The air in the room was lightly scented with some floral fragrance which Tad found quite pleasant.

"Here we are, gentlemen." The woman's cheerful voice interrupted his thoughts, and he turned to look at the little lady she was now speaking to. "Mrs. T, your grandson and his guest are here. We'll send out snacks in a little bit. Enjoy your visit!"

She turned and walked away, and Tad turned back at the sound of a merry giggle.

"Poor Miss Rogers," she said, still giggling. "I really ought to put her out of her misery, don't you think, Zeke?"

Zeke looked puzzled by the comment but only said, "Gram, this is Mr. Meredith, my patient."

Lila May Taylor was a tiny woman, even smaller than his mother, with skin a deeper copper tone than her grandson's. She had a bird-like tilt to her head, delicate features, and a radiant smile.

"Welcome, Mr. Meredith. Please, won't you sit down?" she invited him, gesturing regally to the chair across from her.

"Thank you, ma'am," he replied, "and please, call me Tad."

He felt Zeke's eyes on him, but he deliberately didn't look at him. He was going to do everything he could to show Mrs. Taylor that Zeke had a good and kind boss and he was being well taken care of. He rushed on before she could respond. "I've brought you a little gift Zeke assures me you will enjoy."

He handed her the chocolate sampler in a gift bag and watched as she peeked inside. The smile that spread across her face made his heart swell with pleasure. She looked very much like her grandson at that moment.

"Oh my! Thank you, Mr...Tad! This is very sweet of you."

"It was my pleasure, ma'am."

"My grandson doesn't bring me treats like these," she offered in a stage whisper, as though Zeke weren't sitting right next to her gazing lovingly at her. She turned to him and added, "You could learn a thing or two from this young gentleman, Zeke. *He* knows how to make a good first impression."

Far from being offended, Zeke was amused, chuckling at her as he answered. "I don't need to make a good impression on you, Gram. You already know me."

Tad watched the byplay between the old woman and Zeke, enjoying the love he could almost feel pulsing between them. He loved his mother and had loved his father, but theirs had always been a conservative kind of love, not overly demonstrative, and never with the easy, good humor between these two.

He smiled at the old woman and had to stop his jaw from dropping when she said, "You need to

76

practice on me, so you'll have it down pat when Mr. Right comes along."

Wait, what? Did she just say Mr. Right? Zeke was gay? Holy fuck! He wanted to leap up and dance a jig around the table, but aside from still being a little unsteady on his feet, he didn't want to have to explain to Zeke's grandmother that was the best news he had all day, because he had set his sights on her grandson from day one. That might not go over too well. Schooling his features, because he was forty-two not two, he merely smiled at her, still avoiding Zeke's eyes which he could now feel boring into him. Could he tell Tad was like a kid at Christmas with that little bit of info?

"I'm sure I'll manage just fine, Gram."

Zeke's tone was a shade cooler than it had been before, but when Tad finally looked at him, there was nothing in his expression to indicate how he was feeling about his grandmother having outed him to his employer. Tad could understand how the situation might be a bit awkward for him since he didn't know whether or not Tad was homophobic. He needed to put Zeke at ease, and the best way to do that was to out himself. He had no qualms about doing so in present company. There was something wholesome and stable in the atmosphere around the table, something steadfast and trustworthy.

"I think Zeke could probably school me, Mrs. Taylor, with his ever-thoughtful ways," he said as nonchalantly as he could, "because I haven't had any success finding *my* Mr. Right, either."

This time, Zeke couldn't stop the shock that slid across his face. Tad looked at his grandmother, and she was smiling smugly, like the cat that found the

77

cream someone had tried to hide away from it. He did a double take when she winked at him, though he was sure Zeke didn't notice it. *Wait...had she just set them up? How did she know?* He couldn't help but chuckle and wonder what had given him away. He turned his eyes back to Zeke who was blushing faintly now and apologizing for his grandmother.

"Don't mind her, boss," he said. "This is how she entertains herself...by embarrassing me in public." He didn't sound too put out by it, though.

"Well, first of all, I'm not 'public', and you don't seem too embarrassed. Besides, what's there to be embarrassed about? Mrs. Taylor is just looking out for your wellbeing."

"Gram is just being nosy, you mean, and trying to manage my life."

"I'm only interested in your love life," the incorrigible old lady chimed in, unperturbed by her grandson's words. "And if this good-looking young fella can help with that, I'm all for it."

This time, it was Tad whose cheeks burned with color. He was glad she thought he was good-looking, and he'd take "young" every time. But he wished he could respond with all the words that were crowding against his tongue and the roof of his mouth. Words about his desire to help Zeke with his love life in any way Zeke wanted. Words about thinking Zeke could probably make *his* love life take off like a rocket, too. Words about them sharing their love lives with each other.

"See, Gram? Now you've managed to embarrass my boss!"

He realized he'd been silent a bit too long because Zeke's tone this time was decidedly less affable and sterner as he scolded his grandmother. He hastened to intervene, to clear the air before things became uncomfortable.

"It's okay, Zeke. I'm not embarrassed." He turned to Mrs. Taylor and added with a smile, "I appreciate your frankness, ma'am. It's rather liberating."

Thankfully, someone approached just then pushing a trolley laden with goodies for their snack. After unloading it, the young man departed and Mrs. Taylor took charge. After insisting they hold hands for grace, she continued, "Everything on this tray is pretty tasty, for institutional food," she began, "but these are my favorite."

She pointed to a plate containing cute little triangular sandwiches made with crusty bread and some kind of meat paste. "And all their cookies are delicious. Dig in!"

Tad took his cue from Zeke, who waited until his grandmother added what she wanted to her plate before helping himself. Tad wasn't particularly hungry, but he didn't want to be rude, so he took a sandwich and a cookie and poured himself a cup of coffee, pleased that even though his hand shook a little, he managed not to spill any. Once he had put down the pot, Zeke poured a cup for his grandmother and for himself.

"So, how exactly is my Zeke helping you, Tad?"

Tad looked over at Zeke who shrugged. "HIPAA laws make it illegal for me to disclose health information about my patients to anyone. You're the patient, however. You can tell whomever you choose whatever you like."

Tad nodded in understanding, taking note of another thing to admire about his nurse. It was clear Zeke and his grandmother were very close, and he had not told her what his job entailed was a sign to Tad that Zeke could be trusted with bigger secrets than the fact someone had smashed into him at a red light, leaving him severely bruised and scrambling his brains.

"I was in an accident and in hospital and rehab for a month," he began. "Zeke is helping me with regaining my balance and my memory, and with reintegrating me back into my life before the crash."

"Oh, my dear, I am so sorry to hear that," Mrs. Taylor began, "but it's lovely to see how far you've come since then. And I'm so glad my grandson is helping you to come back to full strength."

"I'm glad he's helping me as well, ma'am."

They finished the snack in silence, and then Tad took up the conversation. "How do you like living here, Mrs. Taylor? Do you miss being with Zeke?"

He noticed Zeke turned to look at his grandmother, as though he was very interested in her answer. Did he like living with her instead of in his own place? Did he even *have* a place of his own? Being over forty, Tad much preferred living on his own, and the only reason he was back in his parents' home was after the accident, his mother insisted his penthouse apartment was not a suitable place for him to recover from his injuries until he was back to full health.

He let her have her way because he knew she would worry otherwise and nag him relentlessly until he either gave in or let her come to stay with him. He didn't want his mother living in his space, and

80

anyway, she was right. He needed to be closely monitored, and even though Zeke was hired to be with him 24/7, in fact, the man had to be given breaks. And should an emergency arise with his grandmother, he might need to leave, which would leave Tad alone in the apartment. But soon, he'd be well enough to be on his own again…

"Tad?" His name spoken with concern brought Tad out of the fog of his thoughts.

"Um, I beg your pardon, ma'am." His cheeks felt like they were on fire. How badly inattentive had he been?

"It's quite all right," Mrs. Taylor said. "I was just saying I do miss Zeke, but as I've told him, he's not to put me before himself. He needs to work, to live, and be independent, and I would never ask him to give up what he loves to do to babysit me."

Tad smiled, understanding exactly how she felt. He detested being coddled himself, knew how frustrating it was, and hated how much for him it felt like an admission of weakness.

He nodded his agreement as she continued, asking, "How soon do you think you will be able to go back to work? I Googled your name and see you have been very busy not only working in your family's company but also serving your country."

Tad hid his surprise at that piece of information and focused on his frustration at not knowing when he would be back to normal.

"I don't actually know, but I'm hoping it will be soon. Anything I don't remember, I'm sure my EA or someone else who works with me will be able to refresh me on."

He pushed more confidence into his voice than he was feeling. Because he needed to believe his memory loss wasn't permanent and it wouldn't affect his ability to do his job effectively. Thankfully, the old lady moved on to talking about his time in the Navy, and while there were certain things he couldn't ever discuss because of their classified nature, he was delighted at how much she seemed to enjoy the stories he *could* tell.

Before he knew it, the time came for them to leave. Tad leaned in and kissed the old lady's soft cheek when she pulled him in by the hand he held out to shake hers. He liked how warm and accepting she was, and knew the more time he was able to spend with her, the more he would come to feel for her. Lila May Taylor was as charismatic as her grandson, and Tad knew he didn't stand a chance against her charms. He stepped away to give Zeke time to say his goodbyes and found himself accosted by a rather frail-looking older gentleman with piercing eyes and a megawatt smile.

"So, Zeke has finally found himself a man to bring to meet his grandma, eh? And a handsome one, too."

He extended a shaking hand to Tad, who took it gently, surprised by the strength and vigor of the handshake. He smiled at the man's misconception regarding his relationship with Zeke, but didn't think it necessary to correct the impression. He rather liked the idea he and Zeke were connected by more than just the job that had brought them together. And as his attraction to him grew, Tad was determined to do everything he could to make the perception into reality.

"I hope we'll see you again soon, young fella," the man said. "It does me good to see young folk coming in to visit. I get to enjoy them vicariously since I have no family of my own."

Tad's eyes widened in shock, not only at the information the man had so casually thrown out there but also at the fact he didn't seem even remotely upset by it. How sad it must be to have no one to visit with you at the end of your life.

"I'll make sure to come and visit with you next time, sir." The promise left his lips before he had a chance to think it through. "I'm Tad, by the way."

"Jim Street, Tad. A pleasure to meet you, young fella."

Zeke appeared at his elbow just then. "How are you today, Jim?"

"As well as can be expected, my boy! I was just talking to your man here, and he's promised to come and sit with me next time. I'm looking forward to that."

Jim leaned in and lowered his voice, which was already pretty thready, so both men had to lean down to hear him.

"You've caught a good-looking one, Zeke. Hang on to him. You know what they say...a good man is hard to find."

He ended the statement with a wild cackle that was choked off when he started coughing and couldn't seem to stop. Zeke led him over to the water cooler, snagging a cup from the table next to it, and got him some water. He helped Jim to sip it and waited until the coughing subsided before dumping the cup and saying, "Okay now, Jim?"

"Yes. Good as new." His voice was raspy from the coughing, but the tone was still one of great good humor. "Thank you." He winked at Zeke as he spoke, eliciting a chuckle.

They were still smiling when they parted ways with the old guy, and as they were driving through the gates of the estate which housed the home, Zeke asked, "What did Jim mean by that comment about talking to my man?"

Tad turned to look at him with a grin. "He thinks I'm your guy. He thinks it's about time you brought home a guy to introduce to your Gram."

Zeke's sigh was longsuffering. "You didn't straighten him out, did you?"

Tad knew his chuckle was a little bit evil. "Where would be the fun in that?"

Zeke shook his head. "Don't you think it's irresponsible to allow people to think such an assumption is true?"

Tad couldn't tell if Zeke was outright angry or just irritated with him, and he knew he was being incredibly childish, but he couldn't find it in himself to care too much. It was an innocent enough assumption, after all. What harm could there possibly be in letting an old man think Zeke and he were a couple? Who was Jim Street going to tell? Unless the facility was a hotbed of gossip that had a pipeline to the media, he was fairly certain they were safe. Still, if there was even a small chance Zeke was mad, he needed to mollify him and get them back on even keel.

"I don't think Jim would be too terribly upset if we were to tell him he'd got hold of the wrong end of the stick. If you feel that strongly about it, I'll tell him the next time we go back to visit your grandmother. Will that be enough for you?"

Zeke pulled his gaze away from the road for a second, his glance calculating. "Why do I feel like you're planning something?"

Tad laughed. "Oh, ye of little faith. I have nothing at all in mind except to make it so you'll stop being mad at me. I prefer the cheerful Zeke to the grumpy one."

Zeke's shoulders relaxed and Tad could see from his profile he was finally smiling. He counted that as a win. He'd have to find a way to make it so by the next time he visited the old folks' home, the assumption Jim Street had made would be real.

Chapter Seven

Mid-August

The night was eerily quiet...the calm before the storm. They had been expecting a major storm since the day before, and for some reason, Tad's headaches had returned with a vengeance. He had been migraine-free for almost two weeks until the weather changed. He had gone to bed an hour earlier after not being able to eat dinner, nauseated, and needing the cool quietness of his darkened room. Zeke had given him his meds, pulled the blackout curtains across the windows and French doors, and had just tiptoed out, satisfied Tad would sleep for at least a couple of hours.

Sheet lightning lit up the sky and thunder rumbled in the distance. It was a low threatening grumble, like a dog growling in warning at a stranger. Zeke went to get his knitting and returned to sit cross-legged just outside Tad's bedroom. The stage was set for him to have a night terror, and Zeke needed to be prepared. He'd knit for a while, and if Tad made it through the first two hours, or through the storm, whichever came first, then he'd go to bed. The last night terror had been hard on Tad. He hadn't gone back to sleep and had been a wreck all the next day, which had made him snappish. Zeke knew how much Tad hated the mood swings that still wracked him from time to time and was glad he was built for patience.

He wondered what Tad had been like in the Navy. Had he been a hardass? He could well imagine it, what with the way he got when the mood took him. He was glad most of the nastiness spent itself on his mother, whom Zeke secretly felt probably deserved it anyway. He stopped for a moment to check his work, redoing a few stitches that were too loose for the section of the pattern he was knitting. Then, as his fingers worked, he thought about the man he was watching out for. At this point, there was little that he needed to do for Tad medically. He was no longer unsteady on his feet, and his ribs were almost completely healed. His headaches and the night terrors were the only symptoms, aside from his still reluctant memory, that were troubling to him.

He really didn't need to be there anymore, but Zeke was secretly glad no one had yet broached the subject of ending his employment. Tad seemed just as reluctant to let him leave as he was to go, and though Zeke hadn't had many romantic encounters, he knew enough to know his patient was attracted to him. Which was both thrilling and terrifying, since he had no frame of reference for how to handle a man like Tad. And yet, he was excited at the idea Tad also shared the feelings he kept trying to subdue. The last time he had kissed someone aside from his grandmother, he'd been just finishing his second year in the two-year college, and the affair had been brief and mostly bland. He had loved it because it had been good in parts and because the boy he had loved had been sweet to him. But they had drifted apart when his boyfriend decided to enlist in the Army, and after a while, he hadn't even received the letters which had been fairly frequent in the beginning.

Since then, there had been a few random dates, a few hot kisses, but no one until Tad had made Zeke feel like he was missing out on what it meant to be in a relationship. He missed a stitch as he considered the lust that never seemed to leave him whenever Tad was around. Undoing the mistake, he corrected the error and forced himself to pay attention to what he was doing instead of thinking about kissing Tad and doing other things with him that he had never done with anyone else. He snorted at the idea of Tad wanting to do anything with him once he discovered he was inexperienced. There was no way the older man would stay interested in a guy who, despite his age, was still a virgin. Men like Tad knew what they wanted and who they wanted it with, and they didn't have the patience or the time to coach newbies in the finer points of seduction and lovemaking.

Time passed slowly as the storm came closer, and Zeke stopped often to listen, making sure his charge was still asleep. Then a sharp thud pierced the quiet after the last, loudest clap of thunder. Zeke stopped working to listen again, uncertain he had heard anything. Then he heard the footsteps and stood quickly, dropping the knitting on top of the bag he stored it in when he wasn't working on it. When he looked into Tad's eyes, it was clear he wasn't quite awake and that he was terrified.

"Hey, where are you going?"

Zeke kept his tone even and low since Tad was only half awake and liable to lash out if he was startled. Tad's tone was horrified, his eyes wild and darting from left to right, as though he could see the thing that was frightening him.

"It was a red truck that hit me. He was going too fast and couldn't stop in time. I saw him coming, and I tried to get out of his way, but I couldn't."

This was new. Usually, Tad's dreams were faceless, nameless horrors that shook him awake screaming but unable to explain what had frightened him. This time, he knew why he was frightened, and he was clearly reliving that nightmare. Zeke observed the trembling hands Tad held fisted at his sides.

"Come on." Zeke took his arm and tried to lead him back into his bedroom.

"I...I...Not..."

His voice was hesitant, his body tense and fearful. Zeke hated it. Tad definitely wasn't all the way awake, and he sure as hell didn't want to go back into his room. Zeke pulled him gently along to his own smaller room and let him in.

"Come on, sit down. I'll get you some water."

He waited until Tad eased his body against the back of the seat before moving to fill the glass that was always on his side table with water from the tap in the bathroom. He brought it to Tad, whose eyes were closed, head leaned back against the seat, hands still trembling slightly in his lap. He was only wearing boxers, and Zeke cursed his own body's immediate reaction to Tad's nearness and the sight of all that muscled glory sitting in his chair in body-hugging underwear. *Fucking inappropriate, buddy!* He gave him another minute, chastising himself as he handed Tad the glass and watched as he drank thirstily, like a parched man in a dessert.

"Thank you, Zeke."

"You're welcome. You all right now?"

Zeke could tell Tad was fully alert now by the firmness of his voice and by the tentative smile that came and went on his face.

"I'll be fine." He looked around him as if suddenly becoming aware of where he was and faint color stained his cheeks. "Let me get out of your way."

He stood up, obviously uncomfortable, headed back toward the door and stumbled. The remnants of the dream memory must have made him uncertain of his footing. Zeke reached out to steady him, and Tad grabbed his arms to keep himself upright. The scent of the man filled Zeke's nostrils...the faint remnants of his spicy cologne and the distinctive woodsy aroma that was so uniquely Tad that drove him crazy on a good day. Now, this close to him, it played havoc with his senses, making him wish he could pull the tempting man in his arms all the way into his body and find ways to make them both settle down. The thought of a happy ending to this encounter made Zeke's body stir painfully, and he moved to pull away from Tad. Putting distance between himself and his boss was the best way to handle this sharp spike of desire.

But it seemed Tad had other ideas. Before he could move too far away, Tad leaned in and pressed his lips to Zeke's, a tentative request, an expression of hope, and a testing moment of discovery. Zeke inhaled sharply, and Tad pressed harder against the seam of his lips, demanding entry. Zeke fought for a moment to resist the dangerous allure of the contact. Fought and then gave in, surrendering to the insistence of Tad's lips on his and to his own awakening need.

The kiss was sweet and needy and hungry and grateful all rolled into one. He let Tad coax his lips open, let him taste his tongue, let him hear the groan of pleasure Zeke did not wish at that moment to deny him. He reveled in it and returned it with equal fervor, tasting Tad in his turn, suckling his tongue for a precious moment, letting the starburst of emotion explode behind his eyes.

And then he pulled away, both of them breathing hard as they tried to regain control. He felt the rumble of disappointment and disapproval under the hand he placed on Tad's chest. He could relate; his own heart was breaking just a little at the loss of contact. It was painful but necessary. The silence stretched between them, but before he could speak into it, Tad said, "I'm sorry, Zeke."

And there it was.

Zeke inhaled slowly, bearing the blow of the expected rejection as stoically as he could. What else had he thought would happen? That one kiss would make Tad want more from him that his agreement to accept what was essentially a gesture of gratitude? *Stupid! You knew not to let him get close to you. You knew, and you did it anyway!* Pushing his self-recrimination aside, he listened as Tad continued to speak.

"I'm not sorry I kissed you," he said, bringing Zeke's thoughts to a screeching halt in their tracks. It was as though he was a mind reader. "I'm not even sorry I may have messed up our working relationship."

Zeke had thought of that from the beginning, which was why he had known getting closer would spell disaster for the two of them.

Tad was still speaking. "I *am* sorry you'll think it's just a fluke because I needed you to comfort me after another night terror." Yeah, he must be a mind reader. "I'm sorry it wasn't enough, and you probably won't let me do it again. I'm just sorry it's over."

Well, there's no acceptable answer to that comment. Shut the fuck up before you make things harder. Pun fucking intended! Zeke cleared his throat, willing his body to stay relaxed and tried for a smile. He could do cool, detached, and professional. He hoped it worked.

92

"It's okay, Tad, as long as you know it can't happen again." He forestalled Tad's protest by adding, "Let's get you back to bed."

He turned away and waited for Tad to pass back into the hallway, following him to his room and watching him go in. He pulled up the set of sheets Tad had kicked off the bed back on, setting them to rights before turning to him again.

"Do you need me for anything else?"

Well, damn! That was clearly the wrong question to ask, because Tad's eyes flared, and he licked his lips, tweaking Zeke's control. Why the hell would he even go there like that? His question sure as hell hadn't come out as he'd meant it...had it? Was his subconscious now playing with his speech, making him say the things he hid from both of them every day?

"No, thanks. I'm good. I'm sorry I woke you."

"It's fine. And you didn't wake me."

He stepped out, closing the door quietly behind him. This wouldn't do. One kiss should not have the power to loosen his tongue and destroy the wall of reserve he had built so painstakingly these past few weeks. Only another week or two and he'd be home free. The night terrors, despite tonight's episode, were far fewer than they had been, and Tad could manage his headaches better now. Heck, in a few hours he was getting ready to go back into work for the first time. All Zeke needed to do was keep his shit together for a little longer. Could he do it? Only time would tell.

Sleep didn't come easy after that. He listened with half an ear for signs of disturbed sleep from Tad's room, though he knew his night terrors only happened once a night when they happened at all. But he couldn't get the feel of Tad's cushioned lips out of his mind or the sweet taste of him on his tongue. And even with his limited experience, he could tell Tad knew what the hell he was doing, he knew how to seduce, how to make a man lose control, how to kiss a man into submission. What would it be like to let go completely and let Tad do as he pleased with him? How great would the pleasure be?

After a while, knowing he wouldn't get any real sleep, Zeke got out of bed and made notes about the night terror. This one had been different because it had, in fact, been a memory coming back to the surface. He could well understand why Tad had been so terrified of returning to his room. Maybe this would be the turning point to him getting his memory back all the way instead of in fits and starts since this was the first real full memory, even if it was just a small one.

The neurologist's appointment was scheduled for the following day after he had his first day back at work, and it would not be too soon. Satisfied with his notes, he dressed for a run and went down, passing Bailey on the way out.

"Good morning, Mr. Zeke," the butler said with a smile. "It's going to be a lovely day today."

Zeke returned the smile, still warmed by how easily he got along with the older gentleman, and how accepted and welcome Bailey made him feel.

"I sure hope it will be, Bailey. The boss goes back to work today."

Bailey looked pleased and said confidently, "I'm sure he will be fine, Mr. Zeke. Mr. Tad never met a challenge he couldn't overcome."

The comment took Zeke immediately back to the early morning kiss and he wondered, as he stepped out into the muggy August pre-dawn, if he was some kind of challenge Tad needed to tame. He supposed it was possible since he had managed, until earlier, to avoid being familiar with Tad, and had refused to succumb to the sometimes really obvious flirtation. Should he take that morning's little encounter as anything other than Tad looking for another win, another accolade, another notch on his bedpost of conquests? The question gave him a painful sense of disquiet, and he ran with the heaviness of it weighing him down, upset he was bothered by the thought of being nothing more than a challenge to be crushed.

Pushing himself harder in an effort to escape his thoughts, he ended his morning jog with some cool-down stretches, twisting his body like a pretzel to work out the kinks and knots. Then he went up to his room for his swim shorts, meeting Tad on the landing and going down with him for their usual swim. The air was strained between them, with Tad barely speaking to him, and leaving him outside his room without a word at the end of the hour.

Zeke went to shower and look through his closet to see what he would wear to Tad's office later, determined not to let himself feel hurt. He wondered where he'd be while Tad went to meetings and did what he loved and had begun to do again from home the week before. He'd take his knitting with him, and when he got tired of that, he'd finish the book he started on his e-reader. He settled on a pair of dark-wash jeans and a cotton button-down. His phone said the time was seven forty, and he could hear Tad moving about next door.

He stepped out of his room just as Tad's bedroom door opened. "Are you ready to go?"

Tad looked smart and elegant, dressed in a gray pinstripe suit with a dark blue silk shirt and matching tie. His wingtips shone brilliantly, and his hair, which he had grown out a bit, made him look even more the part of the sexy silver fox than he usually did. He held a briefcase in his hand. Zeke tamped down the immediate spike of lust that dug into his skin at the sight and scent of him, forcing himself to recall the silent treatment from earlier. Tad wasn't interested, remember? He needed to get a grip.

Zeke broke the spell of tension between them with a question. He would have to make sure things didn't get weird between them. If he acted as though everything was okay, then it would be.

"Need help with anything, boss?" *What kind of dumbass question was that?* Shaking his head at himself, he closed his door and approached Tad. Don't fuck it up, he admonished himself as he waited for Tad's answer.

"I can manage."

Tad's clipped response had Zeke fearing his own efforts to keep things on an even keel between them would be derailed by a mood swing. Tad was clearly upset and still not in a mood to talk. Sighing quietly, he turned and led the way down to breakfast, which they consumed in more tense silence. Zeke excused himself from the table before Tad was done to ask Bailey to make two to-go mugs of coffee for the road. He'd been told the office was a half hour away on a good day, and maybe an extra shot of caffeine would sweeten Tad's mood. Then he went out to the car and waited. When Tad arrived, Zeke opened the back door for him.

"I'll sit in the front," Tad said, still sharp.

Zeke complied with his unspoken order, ushering him into the front passenger seat, and once he was settled, he went around to the driver's side and drove off. He knew better than to argue when Tad was in a mood. The vehicle was his; he could sit wherever he chose. He reached over to switch on the radio but Tad's voice stopped him.

"Leave it. We need to talk."

Heaving another quiet sigh, Zeke waited for Tad to begin. It was probably better for them to clear the air now, and for him to know where he stood, than to let things fester. He was grown...he could handle whatever the fallout of his ill-advised capitulation earlier would be.

"I'm not angry with you," Tad began, "and I've already told you I have no regrets about what happened."

"So why the attitude?" Zeke had to ask, hating how sharp his voice was. He didn't need Tad to know how affected he was by the strain between them. "Mood swing?"

"No. I'm fine. Spooked by the dream, but fine." Tad paused, exhaling hard, and then went on. "I want more from you than you seem willing to give me. I get it's inappropriate, it borders on sexual harassment, you may not even have the same level of interest in me that I have in you, we're different and that can be an impediment. But what I don't get is why we don't change the situation to meet our needs. Unless our needs aren't the same."

What the hell? What did he think Zeke wanted from him? He waited while Tad paused, obviously considering his words. Zeke wished he could look at him for longer than a second, wished he could read his features for signs of where his thoughts were.

"What will you do for money when this job is over, Zeke?"

The change of subject startled him. "I'll just go back to the agency to find a new job. Why?"

Tad didn't answer his question. "Would you consider going back to a regular nine-to-five?"

"Sure. Freelancing is hard when you have bills to pay and people to care for."

Still uncertain where this conversation was headed, Zeke followed the GPS directions, turning onto the highway and merging with the morning traffic.

"Will it be a struggle for you to pay your bills and look after your grandmother between jobs?"

This time, Zeke didn't answer the question but asked one of his own. "Look, I'm flattered you're concerned about my job prospects, but what I really want to know is why the twenty questions. Are you firing me?"

He spoke the question that had formed in his mind as Tad had been talking. He wasn't indispensable; he knew that better than anyone else. But being fired would be on his job record for every future prospective employer to see. That didn't sit well with him at all. And he didn't like that Tad hesitated before replying. Better to get that out there right the hell now. He needed to know what his options were going forward.

"If it's the only way that we can explore what's happening between us, I don't see another way, do you?" His tone was sharp, challenging, daring Zeke to disagree, before it changed into something sad and resigned as he continued, "Unless you're not interested in doing that, in which case, carry on."

There he went again with the suggestion Zeke wanted something different, something less, from him. Damn! And why did he have to be the one to make this decision? He realized Tad was being noble and reasonable and having stated his feelings, it was only fair to let Zeke do the same. He didn't have to like it, though.

"I could resign."

The words were out of his mouth before he had time to consider the wisdom of speaking them. Did he mean them? He didn't know, but immediately he felt Tad's eyes on him.

"You would *do* that?" He sounded shocked and yet almost hopeful.

"Would you prefer that?"

Zeke needed to turn the tables and waited impatiently for his answer. Why was he even considering this? He needed his job; being without it was not an option in the long term. But his gut wanted Tad...and he always followed his gut.

Chapter Eight

August

The second meeting ended after two of the longest hours of Tad's life. He'd been back at work for four hours, and he was more exhausted than he could understand. He hadn't done anything physical beyond walking down a hallway or two to an elevator. But now, he felt like he would collapse if he didn't find somewhere to stretch out and close his eyes. All the information he had had thrown at him over the first half of his first full day back had been overwhelming, to say the least. And while no one expected him to fully take over the reins again quite yet, it was clear they were all hopeful he would be back to full functioning sooner rather than later.

He desperately wanted that, too. At the very least, it would relieve the burden on the shoulders of everyone who was having to share his load. The latest overseas contract related to a client's acquisition of an Italian conglomerate, which he had just begun to work on when the accident happened, had had to be taken over by his partner. Jim was already snowed under by his own pretty heavy load of cases he was responsible for, and Tad wanted to take back the team leadership of the project, but Jim insisted he wait a while longer, until he got back accustomed to the long work hours and the intense concentration required.

His other cases already in progress had to be slowed while he was in the hospital and in rehab, and now he was having to play catch-up. He had another round of briefings after lunch, and Zeke had been waiting patiently all morning, finally making an appearance at noon to say it was time for Tad to take a break.

Tad was in two minds about that move. On the one hand, it pleased him Zeke took his job seriously enough he was willing to interrupt his meeting to remind him to take care of himself. On the other hand, it irked him that he needed Zeke the way a child needed a babysitter. He knew he might not eat properly or eat at all if Zeke weren't there to remind him because his appetite was still sketchy at best, and the doctor had made it clear that eating a healthy, balanced diet regularly was as important as his physical rehab schedule.

They were sitting in his office now, and Zeke waiting for him to make his lunch selection. He glanced down at the takeout menu in his hand, trying to concentrate on the choices. But almost like a puppet on a string, his head went up and his eyes went to Zeke. Tad watched as a slow smile creased Zeke's cheeks. He had no idea what he was listening to as he sat quietly, earbuds in his ears as he knitted, waiting for Tad to make his lunch choice with such quiet patience. But suddenly, he wanted more than the easy camaraderie that already existed between him and this man he had only known for a few weeks. He wanted a deeper connection. He wanted to know more than the surface things about Zeke. He wanted to know what made him tick, what inspired him, what made him go ballistic. He wanted to know what made him lose his easy control, what made him lose himself to passion.

The powerful emotions coursing through his body as he watched his nurse were unprecedented in Tad's experience. He had had lovers in the past; he was not a monk, after all. And at his age, he would know whether any of those men had been even close to the kind of man he wanted more with. None of them had been, not even the two with whom he had spent months in a quasi-committed affair. But this man had managed to breach the wall of reserve Tad always kept in place, despite the fact they were not even in the same social class.

Which was another thing that was playing with his head. Tad wasn't a snob by any means, but he was always aware of his station in relation to others. It had been a hard lesson to learn when he had been much younger, people were too often far more interested in what he had in his bank account than in what he had in his heart. And while the opportunists came from every rank and class, he was especially wary of those who had to work harder for a living than he did these days. They had more of a motivation, to his way of thinking.

Zeke threw him for a loop. He obviously couldn't care less about Tad's wealth and never let who he was be hidden in any way. Even Tad's mother had remarked on more than one occasion she wished he would be a bit of a brown-noser so she could know how to respond to him. It had amused him the first time she said it because he could well understand how uncomfortable Jacqueline Meredith was with someone who didn't bow and scrape before her.

A sound made him refocus on his surroundings. Color rose in his cheeks when he realized Zeke was watching him intently. He'd been caught staring...again. It occurred to him that had been happening a lot more frequently in recent days. He'd have to find a way to take back control of himself from wherever it had gone.

"Something I can help you with, boss?" Zeke teased. He knew Tad hated the nickname, especially now they had come to a kind of understanding about where their relationship could go in the future.

Tad cleared his throat. "No. No, I'm fine. I was just wishing I could remember everything. It's been more than two months since the accident already. When am I going to get back to my old self?"

It was easier to pretend he was upset about his slow memory recovery. That excuse would always distract Zeke from making any other discoveries Tad wanted to keep hidden. Until he was free to pursue Zeke the way he wanted to, he refused to let on how deeply he was already caught in the web of the younger man's allure. He didn't need to feel any more vulnerable than he already did.

"When your brain is ready, it'll let you know, and you'll get it all back."

Zeke's deep voice never failed to send little shivers down Tad's spine and this time, the certainty of his tone made him shudder in reaction. *What the hell?* Moving away to the window, he took the armchair that partially faced it, glad that only his profile would be visible to Zeke from this angle. He had to get a grip before he said or did something he couldn't take back. The things that voice made him want to do were twenty on a scale of one to ten in inappropriateness. Not having any response he could give to that bit of caregiver wisdom and support, and not willing to tempt fate by trying to speak with the way his mouth felt dry, he merely nodded and smirked. Zeke was a firm believer in all things being natural and in everything happening in its time, and Tad would need to remember that.

"So, are you ready with your lunch order?"

Zeke's voice broke through the silence that surrounded them. Tad turned his head, not really knowing what he wanted. He wasn't really hungry, but he would eat anything Zeke ordered, even if it wasn't a lot.

"It doesn't matter. You know I'll have anything you give me."

Zeke's smile made his already handsome face gorgeous, and Tad's breath caught in his throat at the sight.

"All my patients should be as accommodating as you, boss," he said with a twinkle in his eyes.

"Are you sure you don't want to start calling me by my name now?" Tad asked, fighting the attraction.

"It's still inappropriate. And it will stay that way as long as I'm still your caregiver."

"Zeke..."

Zeke's sigh interrupted his protest. "Look, I appreciate you're comfortable enough with me and trust me enough to want that kind of intimacy, but I don't feel right doing it. So even if 'Mr. Meredith' is a little formal, it's either that or 'boss'. Those are your options."

Tad could hear the "take it or leave it" that was left unsaid. He sighed. He'd be glad when this torture was at an end because he knew he could never fully act on the attraction he felt for Zeke as long as the other man refused to even call him by his name. How do you even try again to kiss a guy who insists on calling you "boss" and expect to be taken seriously? *Shit! Now I'm thinking about kissing him again. Fuck my life!*

"How much longer will you be my babysitter?"

That hadn't been what he wanted to ask, but it was something to say to distract him from this latest bit of self-discovery. And besides, it was important to know how much longer his torture would last before he could do something about the need he didn't seem to be able to keep hidden from himself any longer. Zeke smirked, no doubt amused by his "babysitter" comment.

"The doctor wants me to stay with you for at least another week to make sure you're completely able to handle yourself without help. And, if you keep having these flashes of memory, full recall could be any day now. But you don't need me to help you recover your memory. There's nothing I can do about that."

Tad couldn't process his mixed response to the news. He wanted to remember everything about his life, and in chronological order, dammit! He wanted to be able to conduct his business without the need for constant reminders about things he was sure instinctively he already knew. He wanted no more headaches. He wanted to be able to sleep through the night without fear of more night terrors or sleepwalking. But he knew the day those things ended would be the day he lost Zeke's constant presence in his home, in his life. And unless he could find a way to let him know how he felt, Tad was very much afraid he would never see Zeke again, despite his having told him what he wanted between them only hours earlier.

The thought was intolerable. It left a hurting in his chest that he rubbed at absently, which made Zeke look at him sharply.

"Are you okay? Are you feeling pain?"

Zeke's worried question made Tad drop his hands quickly and turn away to look out the window again.

"No, I'm fine. Just..." How was he supposed to explain why he needed to rub the ache away? "It's nothing, I'm just thinking," he ended lamely.

"If there's anything I can help with..."

Tad heard the uncertainty in Zeke's voice, and it touched him this big-hearted man wanted to ease his burdens. How had he lucked out to get such a great human being in his corner? And how was he going to survive without him? He turned back with a smile...he couldn't help it, even as the thought of needing someone like that made him cringe.

"You're a sweet, kind man, Zeke. Thank you. I'll be fine."

He tried to keep the sadness out of his voice. He didn't mind Zeke's compassion, but he sure as hell didn't need or want his pity. And he didn't like the thought of being without him was messing with his mind till he sounded like a helpless damsel in distress. He didn't want to name the feelings he was developing for his nurse because to do so would mean making a silent commitment to doing something about them. And after their conversation this morning, he knew they weren't ready for that...not yet. Tad needed to be completely whole again before Zeke would even consider letting him share all his secret desires and longings.

Zeke's smile was like angel-light, brightening Tad's spirits. He might not be able to share his emotions fully, but he wouldn't refuse Zeke's companionship, and he knew the man wouldn't refuse to do everything he could for Tad. He hated he had not had any further memory flashbacks, though he was relieved at the same time. Reliving that crash scene in his mind had disturbed him profoundly, and he wouldn't wish a repetition of it. He still wasn't sure it was a memory of what had happened, because so very few of the details were clear, but there had been enough to let him think it wasn't a dream.

Forcing his mind back to business, since time was at a premium and he had a meeting in less than an hour, he said, "Choose something light. Maybe soup and a grilled cheese sandwich?"

Zeke stood up, putting his wool and needles away and pulling the remaining ear pod from his ear.

"Sure thing. I'll be back in a jiffy. Why don't you take a rest on the couch? You look wiped out."

"Get out," Tad groused without heat. "I don't need any reminders I'm still not a hundred percent. Time is money. Chop-chop and all that."

Zeke chuckled, not at all offended by his testy words. "You'd better hope the line isn't too long, then."

He stepped out before Tad could answer, his footsteps soundless on the carpeted floor. Tad went to the couch as Zeke suggested and sat back, pulling up the recliner's footrest and settling his spine against the back of the seat. He could feel exhaustion weighing down on him, and he let himself relax. He'd take a power nap and be ready for the afternoon. *It always worked in the past. No reason it shouldn't now.* His eyes, which had drifted shut, snapped open at the memory. Holy hell! He'd remembered something else!

His heart rate kicked up a notch as fresh hope broke through. Maybe coming into work would jog his memory? It could happen...and he needed it to happen soon. Forcing himself to relax, he closed his eyes again and tried to focus his thoughts. What else could he recall about how he spent his working days? Power naps and walks always happened at lunchtime, which meant he often missed a meal. Sandwiches wolfed down at the last minute or numerous cups of coffee in lieu of lunch had become his norm, except when the meeting was scheduled for the lunch hours, in which case he was eating at a restaurant or in the staff dining room. They had just hired a new chef...

"Wake up, boss. Lunch is served."

Zeke's voice roused him from sleep, and Tad opened his eyes, realizing two things at once. He didn't know when he had fallen asleep, and he felt refreshed and energized. He smiled as he lowered the footrest and sat up.

"Thank you."

Zeke handed him the cup of soup and placed the sandwich and napkins next to him on the side table by his chair. He sipped the hot liquid gratefully, enjoying the flavor of it on his tongue. But he was too wired to keep silent, and after a minute he blurted out his news.

"I remembered something else."

Zeke's eyes snapped to his face, and though he said nothing, Tad could feel his anticipation.

"It's nothing major, but I think it's important." When Zeke still said nothing, only looked at him with patient eyes, Tad continued. "I suddenly recalled in the last six months I would sometimes take a power nap at lunchtime to counteract the exhaustion of the long days. Apparently, I just had another one."

Zeke's eyes lit up. "That's great news. Congratulations."

Tad smiled. Zeke always seemed to know how to make him feel better. "Thank you. Now for the rest."

Zeke eyed him curiously. "Do you think there's a lot you don't remember, aside from what you did at work for the month before the accident?"

Tad often found himself asking the same question. "I don't know. I mean, how does a person lose a month? Why wasn't it a year? Or just the accident itself?"

"Well, how did you do today in your meetings?"

"They wore me out. Which was embarrassing, but I guess the lunchtime power naps mean it wasn't uncommon for me to be exhausted before the accident as well. With all the hot air blowing in the room, I'm surprised we didn't all knock ourselves out."

He grinned at the thought and preened inwardly when Zeke laughed. He loved how open and unpretentious Zeke was. Tad could relax with him and be himself. He didn't have to be performance-ready, on point, showing his best face. He knew objectively that was partly because it was Zeke's job to help him relax, but he also knew, after the time they had spent together so far, it was who Zeke was. He had no expectations of anyone, nor did he make any demands of them, though Tad knew he wasn't a pushover, either. He loved that quiet, peaceful spirit because it soothed his own tumultuous one and made him feel protected and cared for.

"I'm glad you're still conscious, boss," Zeke said, still chuckling. "I wouldn't know what to write in my report as a cause otherwise."

The thought sobered Tad. The last thing he wanted was any setback to his recovery, particularly since he knew Zeke was actively looking for other employment. Earlier, as they had been coming into the office, Zeke had asked him a question for which he had been stumped for an answer. He certainly would never ask or expect Zeke to give up his job just so they could pursue the attraction blossoming between them. But Zeke was also right that he wasn't a patient man. As soon as he knew what he wanted, he went after it. He knew that about himself; he didn't need his memories to verify that. He spoke resolutely into the silence between them.

"About what you asked me this morning." No time like the present to get back to that conversation and respond the question he had left unanswered. "I haven't changed my mind about wanting to know you better than our current circumstances will allow. But I also want to respect your need to keep things professional between us for as long as you're still working with me."

Zeke smiled, the relief on his face almost palpable. "Thanks, boss. I appreciate that." He didn't say anything further, but that was okay. Tad needed to finish his thought.

"So, I guess the question really is how soon after your contract ends will you agree to see me?"

Zeke swallowed the bite of food he had in his mouth before replying. "I'm not sure how to answer that without sounding like an eager beaver." He paused, averting his eyes for a moment before returning them to Tad's face to add, "Let's leave it at this. As soon as my things are moved out of your house."

110

"I wouldn't have minded an ego boost," Tad said cheekily, feeling a weight he hadn't noticed before lifting off his chest. "I could handle your 'eager beaver', no problems."

Zeke's chuckle lightened his heart even more. Despite the gap in his memory, he knew he had never connected with any other man like he had already with this one, who made him feel lighthearted, who made him laugh, who made the world seem easier to be in. He would do everything he could to keep him in his life. He just had to get through the next few weeks and weather the complex emotions swirling around in his heart. The thought of being able to live in the same house as Zeke made him at once pleased and frustrated, and the thought of him moving out also filled him with a kind of dread. He would get over the confusion of feelings. He had to, in the interests of having more with the man who had just finished his lunch and was clearing away his trash.

"I'll just get that out of your way, boss," Zeke said when Tad was done eating. "I know you have a meeting in here in about ten minutes. You know where I'll be if you need me."

Realistically, Tad knew he wouldn't need Zeke much longer. In fact, aside from the unusual exhaustion of his first day back after more than two months on sick leave, he felt perfectly fine, despite the loss of memory. He remembered how to do his job, which was all that mattered to his partners. He didn't need Zeke to get back on track physically. He was no longer in imminent danger of falling over and re-injuring his brain, and the headaches were hopefully a thing of the past. Maybe he would be able to get his desire sooner rather than later.

"Thanks, Zeke," he said, summoning a smile. He could do this...the job, the waiting, and hopefully, the new relationship.

Chapter Nine

Late August

Today was the neurologist's visit which Zeke hoped would see the end of his tenure as Tad's private nurse. After the explosive kiss a week earlier and Tad's stated intention to pursue something more between them, Zeke had done his damnedest to avoid spending more time alone with him than he needed to. He no longer joined Tad in the pool, opting merely to sit and watch him, going for his morning runs earlier instead, to work off the energy that steadily built in his veins despite his best efforts to stave off any unwelcome responses. Tad didn't object, for which Zeke was grateful.

Tad had a bad headache on his first night back from going into work, but the meds and rest had taken care of the worst of it. They already had an appointment to see the neurologist the following day, and Zeke had been relieved, because he wanted to be sure Tad was really up to the challenge of going back to work full time. Tad had insisted he was well enough, promising Zeke he'd rest and take things easy. He was glad Tad had taken his advice and foregone swimming the following morning, doing some healing yoga stretches and meditation instead. Zeke had watched him as he bent and stretched his body, and as he sat quietly, completely still, his face raised to the sky, and had let the growing desire he felt for his patient free for a few moments.

He loved watching Tad when he knew he wouldn't be caught. There was such an air of vital stillness about him, a kind of active serenity, like ripples on a pond. At times like those, when Tad was most open, when he was not carefully guarding himself or wearing his public face, he was like a beacon to Zeke. He knew him enough now to know that there were depths to Tad that made him more than just a wealthy international lawyer or a former Navy JAG. And his attraction to that inner, deeper person was growing almost as quickly as the fierce fire of desire to know him in less cerebral, more carnal ways.

"Are you all right, Zeke?"

Tad's voice broke into his musings. He looked up to find his patient's eyes trained in him, a hint of questioning in their depths. What had he missed?

"Sorry. I'm fine. I was just...thinking. Can you please repeat what you said?"

He could feel his face and neck heating with embarrassment and was glad the time he'd been spending in the sun had burnished his already gold skin tone so it would hide his embarrassment. Tad eyed him for a second longer, as though weighing his words, before speaking again.

"I asked if you're ready for today's doctor's visit?"

Ah! For some reason, Tad seemed to be dreading the visit. Zeke couldn't fathom why. Surely a clean bill of health now would make it easier for them to be together, right? Was he dreading the decree because he had changed his mind? Zeke could think of no other reason for Tad to be bothered by the possibility of his being let go after today. And yet, it didn't jibe with the way he had been behaving since his big declaration a week prior. Zeke had caught him looking at him with interest, and though he did his best not to flirt openly, Zeke could see how hard it was for Tad not to do things he wanted to do. The dropped hand when his mother appeared, the half-finished sentences, the covert looks of lust...each was a telltale sign of his continued attraction. He'd have to sort it out another time. Now he needed to answer his boss.

"I'm ready." He tapped his tablet, which sat next to his place setting at the table. "How about you?"

"I can't wait." Tad's response was heavy with sarcasm.

"I'm surprised you're not more excited," Zeke remarked, more for something to say to fill the silence. "This could be the day you're given a clean bill of health."

He looked up to find Tad staring at him, his face clear of all expression. What was he thinking? Zeke wished he could ask, but they weren't anywhere near close enough for that to be an appropriate question. Instead, he cleared the rest of the lunch trash away and said,

"Anything you need before I go?"

"No, thanks, I'm good."

Tad smiled as Zeke turned and walked out, and he spent the rest of the afternoon listening in to the conversation Tad's PA was having with his intern. They were compiling a file on some new case the firm had just taken on. It sounded like Tad would be gone for a while to Japan. Was he ready for that? How would he manage without...? He cut off the question, annoyed with himself for going there. He was *not* indispensable, for crying out loud! And Tad didn't need a nurse anymore. And he had lived quite happily without anyone before Tad. He would just keep doing so.

By the time the meeting ended, it was clear Tad was ready for the day to be over. And his furrowed brow said he might have the beginnings of another headache. Zeke walked in as the other men in the meeting were walking out, none even giving him the time of day. He ignored them as well, going directly to Tad and handing him the pills in his hand and a bottle of water.

"I know you think you can handle this without meds, Cap, but the reason you were prescribed them in the first place is so you wouldn't have to channel Steve Rogers. There's only room for one Captain America in town, boss."

Tad answered his attempt at humor with a pained smile and took the pills, swallowing them and half the bottle of water before packing his briefcase and standing.

"Thanks. Just give me a couple of minutes and I'll be ready to go."

Once they were on their way, Tad leaned his head against the headrest and closed his eyes. If he hadn't taken the pills in time, he'd still end up with enough of a migraine to make him cross-eyed. Zeke prayed silently the meds would kick in soon. He hated watching Tad struggle with the pain and discomfort caused by a migraine, and when it was most severe, it took at least twenty-four hours for him to recover enough to not be totally incapacitated. If he was planning to go on a business trip any time soon, the last thing he needed was crippling headaches. He hoped Tad would mention it at the meeting. If he didn't, Zeke would be sure to bring it up. Until he was released, he was still Tad's nurse, and his health and well-being were still his first priority.

Thankfully, they didn't have long to wait in the front office before they were called back. Zeke sat quietly in the outer office while Tad was examined. Then he was invited in for the consult and listened quietly while the doctor asked Tad questions and made notes on his computer. After a few minutes, when he was satisfied Tad hadn't left anything out, he handed over his notes and waited for the doctor to speak again.

"Well, it seems to me that physically, Mr. Meredith, you're well enough to be cleared for any further private nursing services." He turned his eyes to Zeke for a moment. "You've done a stellar job, Mr. Taylor. Although he still gets the headaches, they seem to be mostly brought on by stress, as I told Mr. Meredith, and will likely dissipate once his body gets back into the rhythm of work."

He turned back to Tad and smiled. "I know this is probably a difficult thing to ask of you, Mr. Meredith, but if you can commit to keeping your stress levels manageable and to keeping up with the meds in the event of a migraine attack, I will be happy to sign off and end Mr. Taylor's tenure as your private nurse. Maintaining the exercise routines and yoga will certainly help with that, as well as the power naps. I'm very glad you've remembered taking those as well."

"What about the memory loss? What can I expect there?"

Tad's voice was pained, and Zeke felt for him. He knew how much Tad hated not remembering a whole portion of his life.

"That I can't make any promises about. It will return when your brain is ready to unlock it. Or it won't." The doctor didn't sound unsympathetic, but his tone was no-nonsense, as if he needed to make sure Tad understood that there were no guarantees. "Has anyone told you what it is you have no recollection of?"

"Apparently I'm missing a whole month before the accident, during which I closed an important case abroad, won us a contract for a new one, met with clients about a merger with a Canadian company, and began to work on a new case in Japan."

"Ah...a busy month then. And you recall nothing about it? Nothing personal, nothing professional?"

Tad shook his head and sighed. "Not a damned thing. The last thing I remember with any clarity, aside from the moment of the accident that came back to me in my sleep, as you know, was leaving for Paris to work the case I apparently successfully concluded before coming home to all the rest I also don't remember."

Zeke heard the angry frustration in his reply, as apparently did the doctor, who hurried to respond.

"I'm sure it must be endlessly frustrating to you to not be able to bring back important things to mind, but I encourage you not to let it upset you. Do you remember how to do your job?"

Tad exhaled lustily. "Yes, thank God!" His reply was heartfelt with relief.

"Then that is all to the good. You can remind yourself of what you need to do to pick up where you left off. Putting pressure on yourself to recall the lost memories might make them permanently so."

The thought upset Zeke, and he could see the anger in the set of Tad's jaw, but he said nothing in response to the doctor's words, so the man continued.

"It's the same as with any other memory that's out of reach. The more you push to bring it back, the further away it seems to get. Then, when you're not even thinking about it, it reappears. You know what I mean, don't you?"

"Yes." Tad's response was tight.

"Then, I encourage you to think of this amnesia as a longer memory lapse, rather than a total loss. Don't let it define how you feel from now on. Don't let not remembering the past affect what happens to you from here on out. As you've indicated, there is nothing in what happens from now on that can in any way be affected by what you can't recall."

That made sense to Zeke, and he hoped to Tad. Still, it must be disconcerting to have absolutely no recall of such a large chunk of his life, especially when everyone else did, and even if it didn't include anything that he needed to remember going forward. Zeke turned his attention from Tad's face back to the doctor.

"I'll want to check in with you again in three months, unless you remember anything else, or develop some new symptom that has you concerned. Then by all means come back at once so we can figure out how to help you."

"Thank you, Doc," Tad said. "I appreciate all your help."

He stood to his feet and reached out to shake the doctor's hand. Zeke also shook hands with the doctor who smiled and said,

"Job well done, Mr. Taylor. Why don't you leave your card with my receptionist?"

Zeke's smile was one of shocked delight. "Thanks, doc. I appreciate that."

He didn't bother to say he had no card, though he knew instinctively, when he looked up to find Tad's eyes on him, that Tad also knew that. He couldn't think about that now, though. He would figure out how to design a business card once he got home. For now, he'd leave his name and cell phone number, and his email address with the nice young woman at the front desk.

He stopped by her desk on the way out, handing Tad the keys and saying, "You go ahead. I'll be out in a few."

He breathed a quiet sigh of relief when Tad took the keys after a second's hesitation and walked out, adjusting his sunglasses over his eyes as he went. Zeke turned to the young woman and said, "Dr. Andrews asked me to leave my contact information with him."

Her smile was warm and open. "One moment, sir," she said, reaching for a small pad to the right of the phone module she worked. Ripping a sheet off, she handed it to Zeke and added, "Just fill this out, and I'll get you added into our system."

Zeke nodded, though he didn't understand what she meant by their system. Stepping away from the counter so the person behind him could check in, he completed what was an unexpectedly detailed little card. It wanted his name, address, email address, phone numbers, and job designation. When he was done, he handed it back to her and she smiled again, "Good luck, Mr. Taylor."

"Thanks."

Zeke hid his shock and walked out, wondering how he was only now, after so many years in the healthcare field, meeting people like Dr. Andrews. Was this something the good doctor did regularly? Would he find another job with this man's help? He wasn't going to wait around for it, since he'd need to find new work soon, but it was nice to know his information was now in the hands of an expert whom he could use as a reference. A second reference, since Tad was his first.

Speaking of Tad, he was sitting on the driver's side waiting for him. He smiled as Zeke approached, and when he slid into the passenger side, Tad said, "I hope you don't mind."

Zeke chuckled. "It's your car, boss…"

Tad stopped him immediately with a raised hand. "Wait…say that again. Correctly this time."

Zeke looked at him in confusion. "Correctly?"

Tad's grin was mischievous. "I believe the doctor just relieved you of your responsibility as my private nurse." He waggled his brows suggestively before adding, "So, yes. Repeat what you just said correctly."

Zeke's eyes widened as understanding dawned. He chuckled. "The agency hasn't signed off on this as of yet…" he began.

"Stop stalling. We're no longer in that kind of relationship, and I'm ready for the next step." Tad paused then held Zeke's gaze as he added, "Unless you've changed your mind?"

"No. I haven't." Zeke had to clear his throat to continue. The heat in Tad's eyes when he'd said the words made his own body warm. "It's your car, Tad."

Tad closed his eyes for a moment as if he were savoring the sound of his name on Zeke's lips. It made him want to say it again to see the fire that blazed out at him when Tad looked at him again.

"I owe you one for that," he informed Zeke before looking away to start the drive back.

Zeke chose not to ask what Tad owed him but settled his breathing instead. The look Tad slanted him promised fireworks Zeke wanted as much as Tad did. He wouldn't deny his excitement at no longer being forced to keep his interest and attraction to himself. And even if he wondered how things would proceed between them, especially as he was ignorant of how to date a grown man, he was ready to learn. More than ready, if the tightness in his pants were any indication. How the hell had he come to the place where just a look from Tad was winding him up?

"How about we go visit your grandmother?" Tad's voice broke into his thoughts, but before he could reply, Tad added, "I'm sure she'll be happy to know you've successfully completed your latest job. And she'll be glad to see you, too."

Zeke had no reason to refuse. "All right, if that's what you want to do with your evening. Visiting hours will last for a while longer, and she's probably already had dinner, so we won't be messing with her schedule."

Tad's smile was knowing. "It's what I want to do. And after, we'll stop for a drink before I take us home. Any objections?"

Now it was Zeke's turn to smile. He understood where Tad was coming from. He didn't want their time together to end, either, but he understood they couldn't move ahead without ending the current situation.

"None. Drive on."

He knew Gram would be happy to see him, especially as he hadn't seen her since his last visit when he had just been days into his service with Tad. He had spoken to her almost daily and was satisfied she was getting good care. But he was looking forward to this unexpected treat. He hadn't planned on going to visit her until after he had left Tad's house, but this was even better than his plan. How cool was it that Tad would think of him at a time when he could be celebrating his clean bill of health! Just something else to admire about the man, something else to make him even more attractive to Zeke.

When they stopped in town at a local chocolatier's shop, Zeke's heart expanded even further.

"Let's see what your Gram would like this time."

The shop smelled like chocolate heaven. It was apparently a local phenomenon, and all the products were made on site. Zeke followed Tad around from one display to another, marveling at the varieties and beauty of the products on show. He had never seen this much chocolate altogether in the same place at one time except in the pharmacy. And clearly, those packaged treats had nothing on these goods. There was even a tasting station where he could try anything that caught his eye. That's where Tad stopped, encouraging Zeke to taste test a few things so he could decide what his grandmother might like.

"Mmm...this one's decadent!"

Zeke looked over at Tad whose eyes were closed in pleasure as he savored the morsel in his mouth. His tongue came out to lick his lips and Zeke stifled a groan as he wondered what it would be like for Tad to taste his lips instead of some sweet confection. And when Tad slid his fingers into his mouth and sucked off the chocolate that had melted on them, Zeke felt his body go hot. He looked away, trying to will away the sudden burst of lust.

"Here, try one."

His eyes flew back to Tad's face even as he opened his mouth to accept the treat Tad held to his lips. Hunger flared out at him, hunger and raw desire. God help him, he wasn't gonna make it through this without popping a boner if Tad kept up what was obviously a deliberate seduction. He may not be experienced in the ways of love, but even Zeke could tell when he was being wooed, tempted, lured into relaxing. And he liked it. He liked knowing how much Tad wanted him because it meant his unending desire was reciprocated.

"You're right...it's delicious."

His voice was cracked with suppressed emotion and he looked away again, not caring that the little old lady who ran the shop was watching them with more than a little interest, the corners of her soft brown eyes crinkling with knowing amusement. He would find time later to be chagrined at the very public display of...whatever was happening between him and Tad, but for now, suppressing the hard-on that was threatening to make a full appearance behind the front closure of his pants seemed like a better idea.

"So, should we get your Gram some, then?"

Zeke nodded wordlessly and moved away, turning to look out the shop window, his hands in his pockets. He heard Tad talking to the old lady but paid no heed to what they were saying. By the time Tad tapped him lightly on the shoulder and said, "Ready." Zeke's body had calmed and he was able to walk out of the shop. Maybe he'd make it through this evening okay after all.

Chapter Ten

September

Tad watched as Zeke and his grandmother reunited. It made him glad he had the idea to start their new relationship with a trip to the elder care facility. He knew how close Zeke was to his grandmother, and he wanted to start it off with her blessing. For some reason, it was important to him she knew how he was coming to feel for her grandson and that she sanctioned it. He knew he didn't need anyone's permission to pursue anything with Zeke, but he thought it might win him some brownie points with a woman whose entire life had most likely been led with very little respect being paid to her by men who thought themselves better than she was because of her social status and ethnicity. He wanted her to know that he was different, that he wasn't like those men.

"Why are you standin' off to the side like a stranger, Tad?"

Mrs. Taylor's words broke into his musings, and he smiled and walked into her outstretched arms. He had never met anyone like her in his whole life. She was like the good, clean fresh air he loved to inhale when he went to the country to get away from the exhaustion and pressures of the city. Or like his infrequent trips to the beach house he had on the island. He returned her hug with a long one of his own, holding her small frame gently.

"How have you been, Mrs. Taylor?" he asked when he released her.

"I'm getting better every day, Tad, thank you for asking." She patted his cheek as she continued, "And I see you're doin' great as well."

"Yes, I am, thank you."

Tad let Zeke help her back to her lounger and went to sit next to her, handing her one of the two bags he held. "I've brought you some treats."

"Oooh!" she squealed like a little girl, taking it and peering inside. "More chocolates from that fancy store in town. Yum!" Looking back at him without removing anything from the first bag, she continued, "What's in that bag?"

"Fruits to go with the chocolates." He handed it over and was delighted when she smiled even more widely.

"How did you know apricots are one of my favorite fruits?"

"I took a wild guess," he said. "I wanted to give you something a bit different from the usual."

"Well, thank you, Tad."

She reached over to pat his knee and then turned to Zeke. "And what did *you* bring your ole granny?" Her eyes twinkled mischievously.

"What? I'm not enough anymore? Now that you have boy toys wooing you with chocolate and fruit? And don't I get credit for bringing him, in that case?"

Tad chuckled at Zeke's teasing, loving the way his grandmother laughed merrily at his words. They were so relaxed together, so in tune with each other. And to be made to feel like a part of the intimate inner circle was almost overwhelming.

He relaxed completely and waited for their amusement to die down, before saying, "Technically, I brought you this time. Let's just get it right, shall we?"

He winked at Zeke as he said it, and surprised a faint flush on his cheeks.

"That's even better news, if you're drivin' again."

Mrs. Taylor must have sensed her grandson's surprise at Tad's teasing, as she answered at once, giving him time to regain his composure. Then she added, "So, since you clearly didn't bring me anything I can hold on to, what's your news?"

"Tad's been given a clean bill of health, so I'm job-hunting again."

Her eyes switched between her grandson and Tad and then a slow smile lit up her face once again. "So, is *Tad* okay with that?"

Her emphasis of his name made Tad's cheeks warm this time. She was a sharp old lady, and it was clear that nothing would get past her. Now seemed as good a time as any to do what he had come for. He spoke into the silence that followed her question.

"Yes, I'm very happy with it. It's a relief to feel whole again physically. I'm just hoping to regain my full memory as well, though I don't need Zeke for that." He glanced over at Zeke for a moment before returning his eyes to the old lady, whose own eyes had not left his face. "And it's a relief to finally be able to connect with him on a different, more personal level as well."

Tad felt Zeke's gaze focused on him, but he kept his eyes on the old lady. He needed her to understand what he was saying and he needed to know how she felt about it.

"Well, it's about damned time!"

Tad grinned. That sounded a lot like approval to him, and the relief he felt was huge, since he hadn't realized until that moment how worried he had been she would not receive his interest in her grandson well. He turned to look at Zeke and saw all the emotions he usually kept well-hidden swirling in his eyes. He wanted to reach across the space between them and pull him into a kiss, but that might be a little too much too soon. Public displays of affection would need to be discussed and agreed upon, and Zeke struck Tad as the kind of person who was inclined to be a very private person.

He settled for smiling at him and handed him the bags so Zeke could put the treats away in his grandmother's refrigerator.

"Thank you, son. I'll have some of that a bit later before I turn in for the night."

"I haven't discussed this with Zeke, as yet," Tad said, "but how would you like to take a little day trip, Mrs. T?"

The old lady's eyes gleamed with excitement at the thought, but she kept a cool face otherwise and replied calmly enough, "Depends. Where we goin', Tad?"

"Zeke hasn't seen my home yet." At Zeke's sharp look, he chuckled. "Well, not the one I live in like an adult without my mother." The all laughed at that. "So, because I'd like to have him visit without feeling like I'm trying to pressure him or anything nefarious like that, how would you like to come with him for a visit on Sunday?"

Tad finally lifted his gaze from her face to her grandson's and saw incredulity mixed with amusement and affection reflected back at him. He quirked an eyebrow and received a sexy smile in return. He bit back a growl and forced himself to look away.

"I'd love to break outta jail for a few hours on Sunday."

Mrs. T was clearly doing her best imitation of a prisoner. Her sense of fun delighted him, and when Zeke chuckled at his grandmother's words, his heart swelled almost painfully in his chest. So many things made Zeke a beacon to him, so many things whose pull he could not resist. He was going to do everything he knew how to make this man his.

They left a short while later, after playing a riotously funny game of Scrabble. The words Mrs. Taylor tried to get away with making were hilarious, and Tad had not had so much fun in more years than he could count. It had never been like this in the Navy with the boys. The relaxed, sweet warmth that was spreading through him as he drove back was something he was wholly unaccustomed to. There had been laughter in those years of service, but it had always been edged by that underlying knowledge of where they were, what they were tasked with doing, and in his last years, how well and how justly he was interpreting the law.

"Thank you."

Tad glanced over at Zeke, whose words he almost missed. "What for?"

"I haven't heard Gram laugh like she did tonight in a very long time. You made her happy. I appreciate it."

Tad resisted the urge to reach for his hand. He wanted to touch him, to connect with him so he would understand Tad meant every word he said.

"It was nothing. I'm sure you make her happy, too, Zeke. She's so proud of you. It's easy to tell."

Zeke shook his head. "You don't know her. She's nothing to you, and yet you spent time and money on her. That's not nothing, Tad. She doesn't have anyone else in the world. Just me. I'm all she's had for years. No one other than me has spent time with her, or fussed over her, or made her feel special aside from me. So, it's not nothing. And I'm really grateful to you, especially since you didn't have to do any of it. Thank you."

Fuck it, he had to touch him. Reaching out, he lay his hand on Zeke's thigh and squeezed, taking a moment to revel in the feel of the muscle tightening under his fingers. "You're welcome. I like your grandmother. She's charming and full of good humor and warmth. I've never met anyone else quite like her."

"Me either, to be honest."

Tad found himself wishing Zeke would touch him in return, but he didn't want to risk having the touch he initiated end before he was ready. He would take what he could get and enjoy the hell out of it. He wanted to know everything Zeke was willing to share with him, and he wanted to spend his spare time with him. Zeke made him feel safe and whole, and he hadn't known until he met him, until he spent time with him, that was what he needed in his life. Money and fame didn't matter. This feeling of connection, of belonging...this is what mattered to him at this stage of his life.

The pub he stopped at was not far from his family estate. He pulled into the parking lot, and when they walked in, the bouncer greeted him warmly.

"Mr. M, it's been a while. How are you?"

"Much better, Sam, thanks for asking." He smiled and gestured toward Zeke. "This is my friend Zeke. Zeke, meet Sam."

They shook hands and passed him into the familiar space where Tad had spent some pleasant moments in the past. It had been a while since he'd come, since his last attempt at starting something personal. That had been a pleasant interlude, though what he remembered most about that man was how quickly he had grown bored of his conversation. It hadn't lasted more than a couple of months, consisting of a couple of hot makeout sessions and, in hindsight, one wild and incredibly foolish night spent in the man's apartment trying to fill the emptiness that yawned inside him.

Why the hell was he remembering that now, here, with Zeke? They hadn't done more than kiss once, and he felt better with Zeke than he had for the few weeks he had spent trying to make something of that failed relationship. Hell, it hadn't even been that. It had been a few hookups with a man he would never, under normal circumstances, have even given the time of day. Why had he brought Zeke to this place? He wasn't that man anymore. He had finally found someone he might really come to care for, someone who made his bones ache and his heart swell with warmth, someone who made him laugh, who made him feel. He wouldn't let the memories of this place sully what he was trying to build with Zeke.

They reached the long wooden bar by that point, having pushed their way through a crowd of laughing customers. It might look odd if he were to pull Zeke away and leave, so he sat next to him instead and turned to Zeke.

133

"What would you like to drink?"

"Whatever you're having will be fine. I'm not fussy."

Tad ordered two beers and tapped his stein against Zeke's when the barkeep handed them over. "To the best private nurse anyone could ever ask for. May your next job be a breeze."

"The last job wasn't exactly a hardship." Zeke's grin made Tad smile. "The patient was pretty amenable most of the time."

A sly grin curved Tad's lips. "Amenable, eh? Is that all? Sounds like a boring kind of guy."

Zeke chuckled and sipped his beer. "Oh, I wouldn't say that. He's as far from boring as a guy like me could ever imagine. He's a big time lawyer who comes from money, but you'd never know it from the way he acts. Unassuming to a fault and a real charmer. Just ask my grandma."

"Sounds like you like this former patient."

"Yeah. I do."

Such a simple statement, spoken so plainly, and the wall collapsed between them at those words. Emotions Tad couldn't name rose and washed over him, and judging by the way Zeke's Adam's apple was working in his throat, he felt them, too. Suddenly, it didn't matter he'd brought Zeke to the bar where he'd gone down in flames. It didn't matter he was a successful lawyer salivating after a jobless private nurse. It didn't matter he was over a decade older. All that mattered was Zeke had admitted to feeling something for him, something that would make it easier to press his suit. He chuckled at the thought of wooing Zeke like an old-fashioned lover.

It wasn't such a bad idea. He could see himself being romantic with the younger man. In fact, maybe that's how he would let this play out. While there was nothing even remotely feminine about Zeke, his vibe had always been old school, and Tad figured he'd play that up. Which meant getting Zeke's grandmother on his side had been the smartest move he had made so far. Now that Zeke was free to be pursued, Tad would set his mind to it the way he did everything in his life. He had made a career out of attending to the details...it had spelled the difference between victory and defeat more than once. Now felt like the right time to deploy those same tactics as he wooed the man whose eyes were taking in the scene before him.

"Tell me about some of your other patients. What kinds of people were they?"

Tad knew he couldn't ask about their medical histories, but he was sure Zeke had stories he *could* tell about their personalities. And he knew it was a great way to help Zeke relax and enjoy their time together in a public place while still getting to know each other.

"Most of the people I've worked with were severely injured. I spent a little time in ICU when I worked in a hospital, and in one of the nursing homes the patients were there because of some traumatic injury. But most of them were really cheerful, despite having every reason to be miserable and angry and even scared."

"Sounds like challenging work. You had to be their rock as well as their nurse, eh?"

"It's why I do this. In my head, a nurse does more than dispense meds and take vitals, you know? When I was in hospital for those two weeks, the nurses were so kind to me. They made me feel like I meant something to them, like I was family. I had my Gram, and I knew she loved me, but she wasn't there in the middle of the night when I woke up in pain or in tears, or when I was scared someone was gonna come and finish what they started."

Tad couldn't even begin to imagine how scared Zeke must have been. Fifteen was really young to be a victim of such a heinous crime. Bile rose in his throat at the thought of a young Zeke hurt and afraid. The urge to hit something overwhelmed him, and he gripped the handle of the beer mug so tightly his knuckles felt like they were in a vise.

"Hey, it's okay. I'm okay. I got through it fine."

Zeke's gentle touch on his fist brought his attention down to where the evidence of his feelings showed white against the brown ale in the glass. He relaxed his grip and raised the glass to take a long swallow of beer.

"I spent a lot of my life in a courthouse," he said, "often prosecuting offenses by men and women who should have known better than to do what they did. Acts of violence against others, especially those based on bias of any kind, always hit me the hardest."

He could feel Zeke's eyes on him, curious, knowing. Was he really going to tell Zeke about Ben? They'd been best friends all through high school, and had come out to each other in the tenth grade. Both had known Ben could never come out to his family. His dad was a Major in the Army, a stickler for discipline, and for men to be men. He would never understand his son loving other men. His mom was a middle school principal and upstanding member of the church board. She would have sent him away to

136

conversion camp if she found out. They managed to keep his secret until he enlisted in the Army. He didn't have the grades to make it at West Point, and his dad was already upset about that. Enlisting in the same branch meant he could at least appease his old man.

It should never have happened. Ben wanted one chance, just one, to enjoy a moment of freedom before he was deployed, and he took it, going out on a date with a guy he met on one of those dating apps. They hit it off, and for a blissful couple of days they were inseparable. Tad hadn't been around to watch his friend's back, and no one had been willing to say what exactly happened. But Ben never made it to Afghanistan for his first deployment. They found him, beaten almost to death in the hotel where he and his lover had been staying.

"Hey...you okay?"

Again, Zeke's voice pulled him out of his reverie. "Yeah...sorry." He drank some more beer.

"Wanna talk about it?"

Tad watched as Zeke swallowed and looked back at him. He shrugged. "Not now. It'd just be a mood killer."

The truth was, though, his mood had changed. And he knew it had nothing to do with his head injury. The hurt he felt, the hatred, the raw rage over what had happened to his friend had never left him, though he had learned to suppress it, to bury it in the dark hole where he kept all the things that hurt him, that scared him, that made him feel helpless.

"Ready to go?"

Tad nodded and drained his glass. "Sure."

He felt guilty for bringing down the mood. He had wanted this to be more like a date than it had turned out to be. He had wanted...well, what the hell did it matter, since his memories had hijacked his good mood? He threw some bills angrily onto the bar top and sketched a brief salute at the bartender before sliding off the stool. Zeke's hand was there to steady him. He knew it was an automatic reaction, born of his time as Tad's nurse. It was instinctive, and meant nothing personal, but Tad still felt heat run up his spine at the touch.

"Thanks."

He stepped away before he did something stupid like pull Zeke down to kiss him in a crowded bar. He was not in control of his emotions, and kissing Zeke now would be wrong. He wanted every kiss to count for something, and this one would just be a way to release the tension his memories had brought on. It wouldn't mean anything, and he wouldn't waste it.

They didn't speak on the whole way back to the estate. Zeke turned the radio on, and orchestral music filled the space inside the car. The sounds soothed Tad's spirit, though the hurt still lingered, but he was grateful to Zeke for trying to make him feel better. He was such a nurturing man, it was no wonder Tad found him attractive. Back home, they walked in to find Bailey waiting for them. He was just taking bowls out of the oven when they walked through the door.

"I kept dinner warm for you, Mr. Tad," he said. "I'll just get everything ready while you both wash up."

They headed up together, Tad ahead of Zeke and parted at Zeke's door.

"I'll see you downstairs in a few," he said, adding before he turned away, "Thanks, Zeke."

"Anytime, Tad."

The words, his name on Zeke's lips, and the smile that accompanied them warmed Tad and eased the hurt even more as he went to his own room. He took off his suit jacket and tie, rolled up the sleeves of his dress shirt and washed his hands and face. He kicked off his shoes and socks as well, opting to go back down in just his bare feet. Zeke was already there when he got back into the kitchen, just about to sit down in the alcove where they ate most days.

"Is *Maman* home?" he asked, taking a sip of the water at his place setting.

"Yes, Mr. Tad. She has already eaten. She was rather tired earlier."

He would be sure to have breakfast with her in the morning. She would be pleased about his doctor's visit, and glad Zeke was leaving. Although they hadn't spoken of it, Tad knew his mother was aware of his attraction to the nurse, and he knew she wouldn't approve of his plan to pursue him. It was a good thing he did as he pleased with his life, and had done for long enough she would also know what she thought would not weigh with him at all. She also wouldn't be happy when he told her he'd be going back to his apartment in the city. It was time to get his life back...well, as much of it as he could recall.

It was still too early for bed when they finished eating, and Tad didn't want to be alone with his thoughts. Nor did he want to be without Zeke's company. He wasn't ready. Would he ever be ready? He doubted it, and the thought made a fresh ache bloom in his chest.

"How about a game of pool?" He went with his impulse. They could share some more alone time before he had to let Zeke go. He knew this would be the last time they spent any time together before Zeke drove away for good.

They hadn't done a whole lot of talking while Zeke had been his nurse, and though he knew superficial things, like Zeke was a champion knitter and sang in his church choir, and he wore glasses for knitting and driving, he only had an inkling of what lay deeper. Tad knew his love and care for his grandmother were the best indicators of who he was at his core. It was why he was a nurse instead of any of the other things he could have chosen to be. For example, why hadn't he joined the military, like so many others in his situation had chosen to do? He would have been a formidable Soldier...if he could have made it. His thoughts went back to Ben and he frowned, not wanting to go back there.

"I've never played the game."

Zeke's reply brought Tad out of his painful reverie. Taking a deep breath, he said, "Well then, tonight's as good a night as any to teach you. What better way to start this new phase of our time together than a friendly game?"

Zeke inclined his head in a gesture of agreement and drained his wine glass.

"Another?"

"Don't mind if I do," he answered.

Once they were set up with fresh drinks, Tad led the way down to the game room where pool table stood ready and set his drink down. He chose a cue and turned to Zeke.

"Choose a cue. Make sure it feels comfortable to you."

Once that was done, Tad spoke again. "Do you know anything at all about the game?"

"I know the idea is to get all your balls into the pockets."

Tad smiled. "More or less, yes. And once you've got all your designated balls into the pocket, you'll need to pot the 8-ball to win."

Zeke nodded. "Okay. But why do you rub chalk on the end like that?" He gestured to where Tad was chalking the end of his pool cue.

"So there'll be more contact between the end of the cue and the ball. Here, have a go."

He handed off the chalk and watched Zeke coat the end of his cue. Then he leaned over the table and said, "So, the cue ball is at the top of the rack; that's the one you use to hit your balls into the pockets. Your first hit decides whether you hit solids or stripes. Let's practice. I'll go first."

Zeke stepped aside and Tad leaned down, lining up his shot. "Watch how I hold the cue and how I hit the ball. The object is to *hit* the ball, not *push* it." He saw Zeke's brow furrow. "Yes, there's a difference. And how you hit the ball determines how many balls you can pocket. The one thing you don't want to do is hit the 8 ball before all your other balls are in pockets."

He sighted down the cue one last time before hitting the cue ball smartly and watching the balls scatter. Three solid balls rolled into pockets, and he set up his next shot, explaining what he was doing as he went along. He played the next turn so no balls

141

would make it to a pocket so Zeke could try his hand. Then he had an idea. Thinking how cheesy a move it was, and how many times he'd seen it played out on television or the big screen, he still leaned his cue against the table and stood behind Zeke, lining up their bodies so he could show him how to hold the cue stick to hit the ball.

At the first touch of his hands on Zeke's, he heard his sharp intake of breath, and felt him stiffen under his touch.

"Relax, and let me show you." He waited, controlling his own breathing even as Zeke's ticked up.

"Easier said than done." Zeke inhaled deeply, and Tad could feel him reaching for his own control.

"This is how you do it," he murmured in Zeke's ear. "Decide which ball you want to sink and then hit the cue ball strategically...like so."

He inhaled the fragrance of Zeke's cologne and the underlying scent of the man and closed his eyes against the wave of dizziness that washed over him. This was going to be a hard game to play...pun damn well intended.

Chapter Eleven

September

Zeke tried to hold himself steady, though everywhere Tad was touching him was burning and melting. Relax, Tad said. Zeke almost snorted. As if he could! Something had made Tad clam up and end their time at the bar, and Tad had not been willing to share it with him, so he had thought their evening was over. Not that he was complaining. The time they had spent with his grandmother had been some of the best hours he'd spent with anyone. And since he knew there were things Tad had not shared and would likely never share with him, he wanted to be sure to savor and treasure every precious moment from now on.

"Decide which ball you want to sink, and then hit the cue ball strategically...like so."

He tried to focus on Tad's words and on the way he was positioning his body. He tried to pay attention to how the stick felt, how Tad set his fingers, how the table felt beneath his fingertips. Anything to help him control the direction of his thoughts. Tad wiggled his hips a bit, then rested the cue stick against the side of the table and used his hands on Zeke's hips and his feet between Zeke's legs to position his body just right. Every touch was electric, every movement intense, and by the time he was back in position behind him, his hands over Zeke's, fingers just so, Zeke was whimpering in his head. The need to turn in Tad's arms and kiss him was driving him mad.

"Any time now," he said too sharply, trying to hurry things along.

The sooner Tad released him, the sooner he could slow his heart rate. He didn't like how scratchy his voice sounded. Especially because Tad seemed to be in complete control. Was he the only one feeling out of breath, like a man about to have a stroke? He tried to slow his breathing, to take deep, calming breaths, but Tad seemed hellbent on winding him up.

Tad chuckled. "Find the ball you want to sink and try to line up the cue ball with it." The warmth of Tad's breath against the skin of his ear sent his body temperature up another degree. "Here, let's try this one."

Zeke let Tad's hands guide his own and they made the shot. The ball rolled along the table and bounced once off the side before miraculously making it into a side pocket.

"Now you try it."

Tad stepped away, and Zeke missed his heat immediately. His hands trembled slightly, so he concentrated on steadying them before lining up his first solo shot. The ball bounced off the surface of the table and slid uselessly to one side, missing all of the pockets. The moment was just the tension reliever Zeke needed. He laughed and turned to look at Tad.

"And there you have it, folks. The klutzy beginner's first shot."

"Try again. Remember how I showed you to stand and how to hold the cue."

They spent the next few minutes helping Zeke get comfortable with the feel of the cue in his hand and lining up the cue ball to make shots. When Tad seemed satisfied he had a better grasp of things, he said, "Okay, let's see how many solids you can sink before you lose a turn."

Zeke let him suggest the easiest shots to take, lined up his cue, eyed the balls and did his best. He managed two pots before he lost his turn. Tad sent four into pockets and then missed so he could get a turn again. Even though he knew this was not really a game, and in a real game he would probably be a complete loss, he loved that Tad seemed happy spending time just sinking balls rather than trying to play a real game. He might never play a real game of pool after this, but tonight, he was getting a chance to see another side of Tad.

"Ready to try a real game?"

"I was hoping you wouldn't ask," he admitted ruefully. "I'm no good at this, and I don't want you getting a swelled head because you won off a gross amateur."

Zeke wondered at how quickly Tad had moved from playful to hungry.

"I already *have* a swelled head where you're concerned."

The words held a weight of meaning that Zeke couldn't miss, and they were carried along by a depth of desire Zeke could barely comprehend.

"Oh, I'm aware," he replied. "But I figured you were controlling that beast."

Tad chuckled. "Lucky for you, I am. But I won't deny myself *this* any longer."

He stepped right into Zeke's body as he spoke and cupped Zeke's face in his hands, pulling him in to kiss him. He groaned as his lips touched Zeke's, and slid his tongue over the seam to coax them open. Zeke let him in, needing the closeness as much as Tad did. He tasted like wine and desire, and Zeke gave him back the kiss he seemed to need, sliding his tongue along the length of Tad's, wrapping his own

145

around it, tasting and sucking, his body winding tighter and tighter as they kissed. He was gonna burst into flames if they kept this up.

"Fuck, you're hot!" Tad's voice was wracked with lust.

"Yeah, I am." Zeke breathed out an answer, wrapping both arms around Tad to keep him right where he was. "I'm burning up!"

"Want me to cool your fever, Nurse?" Tad was panting softly between words and kisses.

"Only if you think you can handle it."

Zeke wanted Tad badly. He had never wanted another man like this, ever, in his whole life. He wanted to feel Tad's naked flesh on his. He wanted to learn his body, to caress and kiss and lick him. He wanted to rub their cocks together, to make Tad cum. He wanted to feel Tad inside him and to sink into him until they were satisfied. But something told him this would be even better if they waited until whatever had pulled Tad from the mood in the bar was dealt with. He ached for the man in his arms, but he didn't want to use sex as a substitute for talking. He wanted his first time to be memorable as more than the time his lover made himself feel better by shagging the virgin.

"But I'm hoping you'll wait until the time is right, too."

He spoke those words against Tad's lips, which had returned from their exploration of his neck and shoulders. He waited for a negative reaction, knowing how his remark might seem like a rejection. He didn't mean it that way, but in Tad's current state of mind, it might appear so. A gusty sigh warmed his lips as Tad pulled away, leaving a soft caress against them.

146

"I hate it when you're right."

He left another quick press of his lips on Zeke's before stepping away. Zeke didn't miss him adjusting himself and knew his own cock was rock hard in his slacks.

"Maybe we'd better call it a night. You'll want to pack before you go. Last swim and breakfast in the morning?"

"You got it."

He watched as Tad turned away and spoke again before he walked out. "By the way, the offer's still open. Whenever you're ready to talk, I'll listen."

He wasn't prepared for Tad to turn back and stalk over to him, dragging his mouth in for a fierce kiss with tongue and teeth, hunger and affection and gratitude all swirling on his tongue as he kissed him.

"I've never ever felt the way you make me feel," he confessed roughly when he released Zeke's lips. "And I've never said this to another living soul...you're special, Zeke. Don't you ever change." Another quick and dirty kiss, over before Zeke could respond, and then he said, "Goodnight," and walked out.

Zeke remained standing where he'd left him, his limbs shaky, his cock hard as stone, his heart swelling with what he was sure was love. He wanted to deny the feeling, wanted to say it was too soon, wanted to ridicule the possibility. But how else was he to codify the things he wanted to do with Tad? Things that had nothing to do with sex. He had never had a best friend growing up. People mostly tolerated him. And those that were friendly only went so far as to smile occasionally or say hello in passing.

Tad was his first real friend, and Zeke held the precious gift of that friendship close to his heart. He had never thought much of the fact he had grown up with just his grandmother to talk to until the moment he realized he wanted to keep Tad in his life. A big part of why was the camaraderie that flowed between them. He was already an easy-going guy, but Tad made getting along with him even easier so Zeke didn't need to try to get on with him. He was open and playful, and yet smart and determined.

Walking up to his room, he thought about how Tad seemed determined to move on from just friends. He was on board with that. He could still taste the sweetness of those kisses they'd shared just minutes ago, and he wanted more. He wanted so much more than hot kisses beside a pool table. He knew Tad was right; he was lucky Tad was controlling his baser urges where he was concerned, because he knew they needed to be patient and go slowly. But the very idea he was making the older man as crazy for him as he was made a grin break out on his face as he pulled his suitcase out and began to pack.

That was another thing he treasured about Tad. He was breaking new ground, getting ready to date an older man who was wealthy in his own right, and whose job added exponentially to that wealth. And yet, Tad had never once made him feel like he was less because he was only a CNA with a two-year degree. Zeke knew that Tad's J.D. was the equivalent of a Ph. D. in other disciplines, which meant that technically, he could be called Dr. Meredith. Maybe if he taught college law classes he'd be called that? Zeke didn't know, but he was grateful that his associate degree in science and his LPN certification didn't disqualify him in Tad's eyes.

148

He emptied the drawers, folding the clothes and rolling them tightly before placing them in his suitcase. By the time he was done emptying the closet, it was close to midnight. He left out the clothes he would wear home, and took a shower, deciding to sleep naked so he could pack everything else into his go bag. Stepping out of the bathroom, he thought he heard a sound coming from Tad's room. He went to stand just outside, the nurse in him needing to make sure Tad wasn't having another night terror. He didn't stop to question why they would return. If Tad needed him, he would be there for him.

For a moment there was silence, and then he thought he heard his name. What the hell? Was Tad calling him? Did he need his help? His hand on the doorknob, he was about to turn it and go in when he heard Tad cry out again.

"Fuuuuuck!"

There was no mistaking the word he was hearing or the tone of voice in which it was being said. Zeke froze, realization washing over him. He knew what that meant. Tad wasn't feeling pain; he needed Zeke, but *not* as his nurse. His own body heated up, his cock hardening beneath the towel he wore. Pulling his hand away as though the doorknob was on fire, he hurried back to his own room, closing himself off from the sounds of Tad's pleasure, yet reveling in the knowledge it was *his* name Tad called when he came.

He sank onto his bed, his limbs shaking with awareness and renewed desire. If he had any remaining doubts about what Tad wanted with him, that unexpected and intimate encounter put it to rest. Tad wanted *him!* The memory of his name on Tad's lips as he groaned out his orgasm would forever be imprinted on his synapses. He lay back, wishing Tad

149

was lying next to him crying out his name as they came together. His own frustrated "Fuck!" spilled from his lips as he adjusted himself and tried to find a comfortable position so he could maybe get some sleep.

When his phone went off, Zeke dragged a hand over to shut it off, feeling exhaustion riding him as he sat up. He had promised Tad a last swim and breakfast together before he left. Retrieving his swimming shorts from his go bag, he slipped into them, went to relieve himself and wash his hands and face, and bumped into Tad on his way out. He could feel his whole body tighten with remembered desire and he did his best to keep the heat rolling through him from riding into his cheeks.

"Morning."

Tad smiled at him almost shyly, making Zeke wonder if he knew he had been heard the night before.

"Sleep well?"

The question popped out before he could censor himself. What the hell was he playing at? He was sure Tad had slept like a baby, while he had tossed and turned, finally falling asleep only a couple of hours before the alarm went off.

"Better than you, it seems," Tad replied, looking him over critically. "Did you have a bad night?"

Zeke wasn't ready to discuss it. He didn't think he ever would be. "Just couldn't get comfortable enough to fall asleep. It's fine. I'll take a nap when I get home." He stepped away from Tad, needing the space to get his twitching nerves back under control. "Go ahead down. I'll be right there."

He bore Tad's puzzled stare and breathed a sigh of relief when he turned and walked away with a grunted "Sure." Grabbing a towel, he followed him down to the pool. The water was warm thanks to the heating system, and even though it was still technically summer, there was a chill in the early morning air.

"Laps today?" Tad asked, walking round to the deep end.

"Sure."

Zeke dropped his towel and turned in time to see Tad dive into the pool, clad only in skin-tight trunks. The black material glistened under water, catching the rays of the sun which was blazing down in morning brilliance. His cock jerked in his shorts. Damn! He was fucked. He walked around to the deep end as Tad touched the wall. He grinned up at Zeke.

"Come on in, the water's fine."

"How much torture today?" he asked, trying to lighten the tension in his limbs.

"Torture? When have I ever tortured you?"

Now, dude! Right fucking now! "Every time you make me swim more laps than I should."

Tad laughed. "Who decides how many you *should* swim?"

"Definitely not the sailor boy!"

Tad dragged him into the pool by his legs and when he surfaced, sputtering, the other man had swum a short distance away, laughing hysterically. Zeke struck out, aiming to catch him and dunk him as well, but Tad was too fast for him and swam off, after a few laps. When Zeke began to tire, he tread water lazily while he watched Tad put himself through his paces. When he had done ten laps, he swam up to the wall and heaved his body onto the side of the pool next to where Zeke now sat. Zeke let him get settled before shoving him off the side into the pool and scrambling back from the edge, laughing his head off when Tad surfaced and wagged his finger at him.

"Remember what they say about payback, buddy!" he warned with a grin. "You won't see it coming."

"True, but at least I won't be out here for you to dunk."

Tad pulled himself out of the water and stepped away from the edge, stalking Zeke with a predatory gleam in his eyes.

"I have a better idea," Tad informed him, walking right up to where Zeke stood passing the towel over his wet hair. He'd let it grow out from the almost bald look he liked best, and the glossy black tresses clearly displayed his Native American roots. He eyed Tad cautiously and passed the damp towel over his abs and arms.

"A better way to torture me, you mean?" Tad winked; Zeke's heart skipped a beat as he continued, "I'm sure you'll enjoy this one even more than swimming laps."

Grateful for the change of subject, he said, "I'm leaving today as well. I have to get the condo ready for you and Mrs. T on Sunday. How early can you get her?"

"I can have her from breakfast time until eight, so basically all day. What time do you want us to be there?"

"Nine? I want to take you all to my favorite diner for breakfast. Do you think she'll be okay with not having a big breakfast till then?"

"She'll be fine as long as she has a cup of tea." Zeke's heart rate picked up at the reminder he would be seeing Tad again soon. "I'll need your address."

"I'll text it to you." Tad moved away to pick up his towel and passed it over his body as he continued. "Time for breakfast. Are you all packed?"

"Yeah. I was up till late finishing it last night."

And just like that, he was back outside Tad's door listening as he groaned out his pleasure. He couldn't stop the heat from suffusing his cheeks, so he turned hurriedly away and walked ahead of Tad, ostensibly to open the door for him. Once he was through it, Zeke beat a hasty retreat, took another quick shower and dressed. Checking to make sure he wasn't leaving anything in the room or in the bathroom, he carried his suitcase and go bag out to his minivan to put them in the back. Then he went in for his last meal in Tad's family home.

Mrs. Meredith was already in the dining room when he walked in, following Bailey's directions. Tad was seating her and he walked around to his accustomed seat across from her and sat down. Bailey returned pushing the cart laden with breakfast goodies. They only ever ate in the dining room when Mrs. Meredith joined them, and the silence was always strained. He braced himself for an awkward silence after her brief, cool, "Good morning, Mr. Taylor", and was therefore quite surprised when she asked, as she sipped the coffee that Bailey had just poured for her,

"How is your grandmother?"

Hiding his astonishment, he replied, "She's doing very well, thank you, Mrs. Meredith, and enjoying her new residence."

"Do you know when she will be returning home?"

What the hell was all this sudden interest in his grandmother? Tad's mother barely gave him the time of day under normal circumstances, and now, when he was leaving, she was discovering an interest in his family? He was sure there was some hidden agenda somewhere, but he didn't feel like trying to figure it out.

"We haven't discussed that."

He stopped, unwilling to engage her curiosity any further. It felt tainted, somehow. He helped himself to eggs, bacon, pancakes, pineapple slices, and ate quietly. The flavors burst on his tongue...salty, sweet, savory morsels spreading heaven in his mouth. He was pouring his second cup of coffee when he heard his name called again.

"...Mr. Taylor?"

He looked up guiltily. He had tuned her out and had no idea what she had just asked him.

"I'm sorry. I was distracted. What did you say, Mrs. Meredith?"

"I asked if you have another job lined up. Tad tells me you've been relieved of duty here."

Was it his imagination, or did the woman sound relieved he was leaving? What the hell? Zeke had no idea why she would be happy he was leaving, since the cost of her son's care was not a concern. Too, he had no idea how to answer her question without sharing details about his life that he wasn't interested

154

in giving her. He and his grandmother had not discussed whether or not she would be moving back home, though based on how happy she seemed, Zeke wasn't sure what she would decide. He chose to answer evasively, hoping she'd drop the subject and stop trying to engage him in conversation. Too little too late as far as he was concerned.

"Yes. I'm leaving right after breakfast, in fact. I'm sure you must be happy he's well again," he added, to throw her off her game and get out of answering her question.

If there was one thing he had discovered, it was that Jacqueline Meredith, for all her faults, loved her son and would go anywhere a conversation led if it had to do with him.

"I am, indeed, Mr. Taylor, and I am very grateful to you for helping him to heal."

He looked up from his plate again, hoping he had managed to disguise his shock at her words. Who was this woman and what had she done with Tad's mother?

"I'm very glad I could help, ma'am." If she could be polite, so could he.

"I'm feeling well enough to go home, too."

The mood change was swift as she turned her eyes to her son's face. Zeke breathed a sigh of relief, and promised himself to thank Tad for taking the heat off him. He tried not to listen in as mother and son argued back and forth, albeit politely, about Tad's leaving, and excused himself as soon as he could, going to find Bailey in the kitchen.

"Would I be able to get some coffee to go, Bailey?" he asked.

"Already done, Mr. Zeke." Bailey went to fetch the car mug that Zeke used and handed it to him. "Fixed just the way you like it, too." He smiled warmly at Zeke.

"Thanks." Zeke took the mug, raising it in acknowledgement and turned at the sound of Tad's voice behind him.

"I see you're ready to go. Thank you for everything."

Tad strode forward, his hand extended. Zeke shook it, feeling the way Tad squeezed his own before releasing him. He wished he could pull him in for a hug, but what with Bailey standing right there and Tad's mother trailing behind him, Zeke knew that wouldn't happen.

"Just doing my job. Take care of yourself."

He raised a hand in farewell and walked out through the garage to his minivan. Tad followed him, waiting until he was in the driver seat before closing the door and leaning in when he wound the window down.

"How long before you get home?"

"About thirty minutes if traffic cooperates."

"I'll text you the information later. Drive safe."

"Thanks. And you take care."

Zeke had always hated goodbyes, but something about this one had his insides feeling loose, like his intestines were free falling inside him. It was weird, since he knew he'd see Tad again the next day. He smiled and Tad stepped back, but not before Zeke saw the way his eyes lingered on the lips he wished Tad had kissed one last time. Raising a hand in farewell, he drove off, his sigh mingling with the warm air flowing through the cab. He switched on the radio and lost himself in the country tunes.

By the time he got home, he was feeling a little less like he was breaking apart inside. Still amazed by how upset leaving Tad had made him, he went next door to get Punkin, whose mighty dog enthusiasm knocked him to his knees. He laughingly endured the doggie kisses and made goo-goo gah-gah sounds at the little creature, who yipped and licked his face in absolute glee.

"Yes, I'm happy to see you too, Punkin!"

He chuckled when the dog sat on his lap, then stood again immediately so he could wag his little tail end in utter glee. He felt really bad he hadn't spent more time with him while he had been at Tad's, although it would not have been wise, especially in the early days to spend any time away from him. He had come to see the dog once a week, when he came to check the house and pay his neighbor for dog sitting, but clearly it hadn't been enough. And now, as he managed to get back to his feet with the happy pup in his arms, he wondered if maybe he could take the dog with him the next day so Gram could spend some time with him as well.

Which reminded him of his last conversation with Mrs. Meredith. Although the facility where Gram now lived allowed pets, they hadn't really revisited the question of what to do about Punkin, because they hadn't talked about whether or not Gram was coming back home. He knew she could live there until she passed, but he didn't know how he felt about that. To be honest, he didn't know *how* to feel. He'd lived his whole life with her, and while the thought of living on his own seemed daunting, it was also strangely thrilling.

Here he was twenty-seven years old, and he had never been on his own. How the hell did he think he could handle a boyfriend if he didn't even know how to be a single man living alone? He had none of the self-possession or assurance Tad had, never mind the experience to pull off a serious relationship. Still, he wasn't one to quit before he began, and no matter how much the thought scared him, he wasn't going to back away from this new experience.

Back in his own house, he set the dog down, filled his bowl with water and gave him a treat before setting about unpacking. He made a load of laundry and then went into the kitchen to see what he'd need to get when he went grocery shopping later. As he was adding onions and garlic to the list, his cell phone dinged. Reaching for it, he saw it was Tad. The smile that bloomed on his cheeks was as automatic as breathing. The message was his address and a sad face after the words *Missing you*.

Wow! This was what it was like to be wanted by another person, to matter to someone other than a parent. His insides shook with sweet joy and that shaking made it hard for him to send back the few words he could manage. *Thanks. Me too.*

You miss you too?

A laughing emo accompanied that message, easing the nerves which had beset Zeke a moment before. He chuckled as he replied, his hands steadier this time.

I'm very missable, yes. But that's not what I meant. He paused for a moment, then recalled he needed to ask about Punkin. *I have a question.*

158

His phone rang a second later. "A question about?"

Jesus, he was going to combust with excitement at the sound of Tad's voice after only...two hours? *What the fuck? Get a grip, Taylor!*

"Ah...about Gram's dog. She hasn't seen him since she's been in the home. I was wondering if it would be okay to bring him along tomorrow?"

"What kind of dog is it?"

"He's a pug. His name is Punkin."

Tad's rich laugh made warmth slide through Zeke's veins like syrup over pancakes. He wanted to roll in it, which he admitted was disturbing even as he reveled in the feeling.

"Picture?"

Refocusing his attention on Tad's words, he looked around and found the dog curled up in his bed by the back door. He took a picture and sent it, then grinned when Tad said,

"Cute pooch. Sure, bring him along. He'll be alone, though. I don't have any pets."

"He peoples well," Zeke joked, "especially when they fawn all over him.

"I'll bear that in mind. Did you have to pay dog sitting fees while you were with me?"

"I paid my next door neighbor's teenager to care for him, but it wasn't as expensive as taking him to a kennel."

"Still, I should reimburse you."

Zeke frowned. This wasn't what he wanted. "Don't be ridiculous," he said before he could censor his response. "I was paid enough to pay my bills. I'm fine."

A short pause on the other end, as though Tad were trying to figure out how to respond to that. Then he spoke, changing the subject.

"What are you doing now?"

Glad that he didn't sound upset at his tone, Zeke replied, "Making a list. I have to go grocery shopping in a little while. What are *you* doing?"

"Packing. After you left, my mother and I got into it because if it were up to her, I'd never leave home again, even though I have my own." He sighed. "She's getting worse with this over-protective stuff, and it's driving me insane. She seems to think I'm going to keel over and hit my head again and forget everything this time."

"Cut her some slack," Zeke said, understanding her worry even as he also understood Tad's frustration. "She loves you."

"Yes, she does." Another sigh and then he said, "I'd best get a move on before she marshals any other arguments for why my staying here is the better plan. See you tomorrow."

"Yeah." Zeke smiled widely. "Tomorrow."

Not a second after he hung up, the phone rang again. "Yeah."

"I forgot to ask. Why don't you let me do all the driving tomorrow? I'll come get you, then we'll get your grandma, and go to the diner directly from the home?"

"You don't have to..."

"I know that. But I want to. Maybe I want to spend some time with you alone, before we get your Gram." Tad's voice had gone all growly and dark.

Zeke's skin heated. "Sure. If it'll make you happy. I'll text you the address."

"Thanks. See you then."

Joy and anticipation and a smidgen of fear all bubbled inside Zeke as he hung up and sent Tad a text message with his address.

Chapter Twelve

September

Anticipation was a poor bedfellow. Tad tossed and turned all night, unable to fall asleep until well past midnight. His condo felt like an alien space when he had made it back the day before. Nothing felt familiar when he had first walked in, as though it was a brand new, unlived-in space. He'd spent an hour trying to get that sense of home back without success until he had seen it on the door of the refrigerator...a business card from the local animal shelter with a name handwritten beneath the director's number. A cat...he remembered it was a cat he had been looking at when he'd been feeling so alone.

The weight of the memory hit him hard enough that he slumped against the kitchen island and took deep breaths to steady himself. Then he slid into a chair at the kitchen table and rested his head on his forearms, letting the memory wash over him. His mother had been on him in recent times about his single status, asking when he was going to bring someone home, and bemoaning the fact she was still without a grandchild.

"*Maman*, you do realize I may never find someone I care enough about to marry, let alone have children with, right?"

"You certainly won't find anyone with that attitude, *mon cher*."

"And are you prepared for me to bring home a husband instead of a wife?"

He had felt the need to remind her yet again that he was bisexual and was as likely to bring home a man as a woman. His reminder hadn't gone over well.

"I'm sure you just haven't met the right woman as yet. And if you keep pushing the idea of a husband into the equation, you'll definitely turn off any woman looking for a husband. Is that why you're doing this? So no marriage-minded woman will approach you?"

It was an old argument between them, and he'd been tired of it. She was right that he was lonely and if he didn't watch out, he'd end up a miserable old curmudgeon. Maybe he needed a pet. A dog would be great, but they were very high maintenance, and he was too busy of a man to have time for a dog. Maybe a cat...they were much more self-sufficient, and he wouldn't need to walk it if he got one.

As he came fully awake, Tad savored the happiness that still percolated inside his chest at having remembered something else from the period of his life locked away in his memories. He hoped this meant the rest of his memory of that time would return soon, though he tried not to set his hopes on it. He'd been fine without them so far. He was sure he'd remain so, whether or not he got them all back. He wondered what had triggered it as he stumbled to the bathroom to take care of business. He needed to get in his workout before he had to go get Zeke and his grandmother, and their dog Punkin.

That was it...that had probably been the trigger. And the anticipation at seeing Zeke again had only added to the feelings of euphoria. Finally, he had felt like he belonged in the pristine apartment. He had been looking forward to adopting the beautiful calico cat, knowing somehow she would make his empty apartment full of life. He called the shelter, eager to get the ball rolling again, and explained why he hadn't called back.

164

"I'm sorry to hear that, Mr. Meredith," the perky young receptionist had said, "but it's nice to have you back, sir. Sadly, Kitty was adopted about a week ago."

"That's too bad. I'll have to come back to see if any other cat catches my fancy, then."

It would certainly be a great excuse to spend more time with Zeke...maybe a date. They'd go cat-shopping and then have lunch or something.

"That'll be fine, Mr. Meredith. We look forward to seeing you soon."

He washed his face and swished mouthwash around before changing into his swim trunks. The gym on the first floor of the building would still be empty this early on a Sunday, for which he was grateful. He smiled at the security man at the front desk as he walked by, and once in the pool room, he swam laps until his muscles burned and he was out of breath. Then he did some yoga stretches to cool down, thinking back to the mornings he'd spent working out with Zeke. Ridiculous as he felt, he missed him; he'd be so happy to see him again.

By the time he was following the GPS directions to Zeke's house he was a bundle of raw nerves. The classical music piping into the car did nothing to ease the tightness in his chest or the tension that had him fisting the steering wheel as if his life depended on it. Today would be the beginning of the next stage of his life, the one where he would be open about who he wanted, where he would pursue him without fear. And maybe, just maybe, he'd be lucky enough to win him completely.

Zeke's house was a pretty bungalow in a subdivision of cookie cutter houses too close to each other. If anyone sneezed, his neighbor was sure to hear. The neighborhood felt cozy, and the streets were clean, the sidewalks dotted with the odd tree here and there. Most of the houses sported matchbox-sized lawns, though one or two had well-maintained gardens to the side as well. Zeke's house had a larger stretch of lawn with large, rustic planter boxes at the edges filled with beautiful flowers. Zeke's minivan was parked inside the open garage, which was pristine.

Tad pulled up behind Zeke's van on the driveway and stepped out. A dog's excited barking broke the silence of the Sunday morning air, and he turned to see where the sound was coming from. A wrinkle-faced pug, perched on the window seat of a bow window, was barking madly at him. Tad made his way to the door next to the bow window as the garage door slid downward and rang the bell, a grin creasing his cheeks at the sight of the dog spinning in circles of anticipation on the seat. Heavy footsteps heralded Zeke's approach, but nothing prepared Tad for the sight of him, his hair falling into his eyes as he dragged a shirt over his head.

"Fuck!"

After only twenty-four hours apart, the sight of his man—yeah, that's who Zeke was to him—hair damp and half-dressed, would forever be imprinted on his brain as a turn-on. The shirt had a college logo emblazoned on it, and as he stepped aside so Tad could enter, he tucked it into the waistband of his jeans, which was undone. Tad swallowed a groan at the sight of the waistband of his boxers and looked down. His feet were bare and even that was sexier than bare feet had any right to be.

"Fuck!"

The exclamation was ripped from his lips a second time before he realized he had spoken it aloud. He barely restrained himself from grabbing Zeke to plant a kiss on those full lips. Instead, he cleared his throat and looked away from the temptation that was Zeke's body, now fully clothed except for his feet, glad that apparently Zeke hadn't heard him.

"Morning. Sorry I'm late. Punkin wouldn't go, and I don't want any accidents in your car, so I had to wait on him."

"No problem." Tad latched on to the comment gratefully. Anything to keep him occupied, so he wouldn't fixate on the man speaking again.

"Have a seat." Zeke gestured to his left, and Tad moved into the living room where the dog was now silently watching them from his perch on the window seat. "I'll be with you in a jiff. Everything's ready for Punkin. I just need to get him in the carrier."

"Take your time."

Tad smiled at him and watched him walk out before taking a seat in the big leather armchair by the fireplace. Punkin immediately jumped off the window seat and onto his lap, sniffing him and eventually licking his face before settling down to wait for his master. Tad chuckled. Apparently, he passed muster with the dog.

"You're a friendly little pooch, aren't you, fella?"

Punkin eyed him imperiously, not deigning to respond. Tad stroked the dog's side while he waited, taking in the elegant room he sat in. It was small but spotless and colorful, and he could tell immediately it would be one of Zeke's Gram's favorite rooms. The stamp of her personality was everywhere, from the colorful purple curtains at the windows that contrasted regally with the champagne-colored walls to the coral cushions and gold throws that adorned the purple sofa and loveseat. The rug beneath the glass coffee table was a rich brown addition to the charm of the room. Tad could almost imagine her sitting in the loveseat with her knitting, entertaining her friends with tea and chocolates. The thought made him smile.

"Okay. I'm ready." Zeke grinned at the sight of Punkin in residence on Tad's lap. "I see you've made another conquest. Wanna bring him? I'll put him into the carrier when we get outside."

Zeke picked up a small go bag which Tad assumed had dog treats and such. He nodded, picking up the dog, and followed Zeke out the door. He unlocked the car and let Zeke go past him so he could open the back door. He handed over the pooch and went around to the driver's side.

Once Zeke was settled next to him, he backed out and said as they drove off, "You've got a cute little house, from the little I've seen."

"Thanks. I know it's nothing like the McMansion your family owns, but it's ours, and we love it. Sorry I didn't give you the grand tour." Zeke smiled as he said that, making Tad chuckle.

"No probs." Tad was actually happy he hadn't had the tour. "It'll give me a reason to come in with you when I drop you back home tonight."

"Sneaky bastard, aren't you?"

Zeke didn't sound particularly bothered by that, which amused Tad. It also pleased him Zeke the regular guy was relaxed enough to call him names. He'd take this guy over Zeke the nurse every time. This guy he could flirt with; this guy he could tease;

this guy he could dream about and make those dreams come true.

"I'm a strategist," he admitted. "I wouldn't win quite so many cases or secure as many contracts if I didn't plan carefully and take advantage of every opportunity."

"So, you're saying my not giving you the tour was all part of *your* plan?" Zeke snorted disbelievingly.

"No, smartass." Zeke's chuckle wound its way under his skin. "I'm saying you're not giving me the tour made it possible for me to plan my next move."

"Happy to oblige then," he remarked, still chuckling. "So, where are we going for breakfast?"

The change of subject didn't escape Tad, who smiled widely, though he didn't remark on it. Zeke might feel a bit more relaxed with him, but he wasn't trying to push the flirting. That would all be on Tad for now, it seemed, and he had no objections to make.

"Ever heard of Cee Bee's On the Ocean?"

"Who hasn't?" Zeke turned to look at him for a moment. "It's a bit far for breakfast, isn't it?"

"It's a nice ride along the shore. I figure your Gram will like the scenery, and we can eat on the patio when we get there, so she can see and smell the ocean, too."

"Gram will definitely love that. Thanks for thinking of it." He was suddenly serious and earnest.

"Any time. I thought it would be a nice date for us and a nice day out for her. Then we can make her a fancy meal in a high rise apartment where she can have views of the entire city. Memories to hold on to, for both of you, I hope."

Zeke didn't respond at once, but Tad could almost hear the wheels turning as he thought hard about whatever it was he wanted to say. Tad let him think. He didn't need an answer. He had made up his mind that this man would be his, and he would pull out all the stops to make his seduction more than about the wild sex he wanted to have with Zeke as often as he could. He wouldn't deny his need, but he would channel it, use it to fuel his purpose, which was to make sure Zeke understood, every time they were together, that this was about winning his heart. He would make every moment they spent together an occasion worth remembering.

"This is a date, huh?" When Tad glanced at him and nodded, he smiled. "With my Gram as a chaperone? What...you don't trust yourself with me?"

His eyes fell to Tad's lips as though he knew what Tad had been wanting to do from the moment he opened the door. Maybe he wanted it, too. A guy could hope, no?

Tad chuckled. "Smart man! I knew there was a reason I liked you." He grinned when Zeke's cheeks warmed at the compliment. "I'm prepared to be patient a little longer. And your Gram will help with that."

Mrs. T was waiting for them when they arrived, dressed smartly in a pretty color-block dress, her short hair covered by a rakishly tilted beanie to match the orange, gold, and black dress. A heavy gold choker circled her neck, and she gripped her sturdy cane tightly as she approached with Zeke, who had gone in to get her. She looked fantastic, and the smile on her face said she was excited to be going out. *Age really* was *just a number with this lady!*

170

"Good mornin', Tad! Thanks for the day out!"

"Morning, Mrs. T. You look fabulous!"

She reached up to pull him in for a kiss to his cheek. "Well, I didn't want to be a slouch, not when I'm goin' on an all-day date with two handsome young men, now did I?"

She winked and chuckled, and Tad joined her. Zeke shook his head with a smile. "Gram, where do you want to sit?"

"In the back, of course. I'm not about to usurp you position next to your young man! Besides," she continued, ignoring the startled looks on both their faces to look into the car, "I see my baby's here, and I'm going to need a little time to hug on him before we reach the diner."

Zeke helped her into the back seat and made sure she was properly strapped in. Then, while he went around to the passenger side, she freed her pug from the carrier and had a lovely reunion.

"Comfy?" Tad looked back to her in the rearview mirror.

"Yes, thank you, young man."

He nodded and turned to Zeke. "Put something on your Gram will enjoy." He gestured to the radio as he drove off, and for the next forty-five minutes, they listened to oldies from the fifties and sixties. Zeke seemed to know all the lyrics, and even harmonized beautifully on some of them.

"You sing in the choir, don't you?" Tad asked as they cruised down the shore highway.

"Yes. Baritone."

"I'd love to hear your choir."

Even if it meant stepping inside a church, Tad was ready to do it. That would be far outside his comfort zone, but it was important to him to connect with Zeke in every way. He had known, from the first day they met, that he wanted to know Zeke much better than a nurse should know his patient. And his experience taught him the only way to do that was to share in everything that was important in Zeke's life...well, everything he could.

"Church doors are open every Sunday morning," Zeke said. "You're welcome to come with me."

"So, you're playing hooky today, huh?" Tad asked laughingly.

Zeke chuckled. "I don't go every Sunday, especially when I'm working, and no one expects it."

"I'll bear that in mind."

The rest of the ride was made in silence only broken by Zeke's soft singing and his grandmother quietly humming in the back seat. It calmed something inside Tad to listen to them, and before long he was tapping his fingers to the rhythm of the songs. There was an almost spiritual mood in the car, and he liked it a lot. Eventually, he turned off the highway down the ramp that would take them to the diner and once they were parked, he helped Mrs. Taylor out of the car. He scooped up her dog while Tad took her arm and escorted her into the diner.

"We'd like to sit on the patio if there's room?"

The hostess smiled politely at Tad and picked up three sets of cutlery. "This way please, sir."

Eventually, they were all settled in at a cozy table for four as close to the beach as they could get. The sound of the waves and the screech of seagulls brought a smile to Tad's lips. This was how he wanted to relax with Zeke...on the beach with nothing to worry about.

A server approached a moment later. "Good morning, I'm Bella, and I'll be your server for the day. Would you like to start with some coffee?" she asked with a bright smile.

"What kind of tea do you have, young lady?"

Tad checked out his breakfast options while Mrs. Taylor decided on what kind of tea she wanted. He and Zeke asked for a carafe of coffee between them, and once the breakfast orders were made, they sat back to enjoy the peaceful morning. The restaurant was filling up nicely, including the patio where they sat, but Tad didn't mind. Being outdoors felt much less confining than being inside would have been, even as the tables filled up around them. He watched as a couple walked slowly along the beach, hand in hand, and looked over to find Zeke also watching them. And when he felt eyes on him, he knew even before he looked that Mrs. Taylor was watching him.

"Is everything all right, Mrs. T?" he asked, uncertain of the reason for her scrutiny.

She smiled quietly and nodded. "Everything is perfect, Tad, thank you. At last."

He wasn't sure what the end of that statement meant, but he returned her smile and looked up to see the server approaching with their drinks.

"Your food will be out shortly. Would you like anything else?"

"Not right now, thank you." Tad spoke for the others, nodding his thanks when Zeke poured his coffee. "This is always good coffee," he said, adding his fixings.

Zeke took a sip, then raised a brow in agreement. "You're right. It's delicious."

"This tea is better than what they serve at the home, but not as good as the ones I used to buy when I was livin' with Zeke."

Tad turned to her with curious eyes. "Are you ready to go back home, Mrs. T? I was there briefly this morning, and it's lovely. I see your stamp on it, and I can imagine you must miss being there."

"I do," she said wistfully, sipping her tea delicately, "but I like it where I am as well. I'm not alone with just Punkin for company, and Zeke doesn't have to worry if I take a turn for the worse because there's a nurse and doctor on duty at all times. I'm blessed to be able to live there."

Tad didn't want to pry, but he remembered his mother's question to Zeke the day before about where his Gram would live, and now it seemed she was torn. He looked across at Zeke, wondering what he was thinking about it.

"What does your gut say, Gram?" he asked. "You know how you always tell me to go with my gut, because it's usually the smarter decision."

The old lady smiled. "Throwin' my words back at me now, are you?"

Zeke grinned. "What can I say? You taught me well!"

Their food came before she could reply, and she waited until the server had left and they helped themselves to what they wanted from the common platters before saying, "The home allows pets, so if I

174

stay, I'll be able to keep Punkin with me. I would be moved to an apartment, instead of being in the clinic section. The cost would be more, and I worry you would have to make up the difference. I don't want to…"

Zeke stopped her mid-sentence, his eyes dark with emotion. "Gram, if you want to live there, don't let the cost be a deterrent. We've always managed, haven't we?"

Tad got the impression there was more Zeke wanted to say, but he understood not wanting to discuss such a private matter in front of a stranger. He hurried to change the subject, feeling guilty for having been the reason they were even discussing it to begin with.

"I'm sure whatever you decide, it will be a good choice, Mrs. T."

Zeke shot him a grateful glance and he smiled and nodded. "After breakfast, maybe we can go for a little walk?"

"As long as it's not in the sand. I don't think I'm ready for sand just yet."

"The boardwalk will be better, as we can window shop." Tad was all for anything to make her happy and get her mind off what was most likely a very difficult decision.

"And maybe I can take back a souvenir or two for my friends," her eyes lit up at the prospect.

"That's a good plan. As is this omelet." He changed the subject again, hoping to completely distract her and Zeke.

Zeke cut a piece of his everything-and-the-kitchen-sink omelet and passed it to his Gram who

175

smiled and moaned when she tasted it. Then she passed a bit of her spinach-and-mushroom omelet to him and Tad watched as his eyes widened in shock.

"Gram, that's better than I thought it could be, seeing as it's got fungus in it."

Mrs. T smacked her grandson on the arm. "Stop it! You make it sound like I'm eating something germy."

Zeke snickered. "Sorry, Gram," he said, not sounding sorry at all.

They finished breakfast, had a second cup of coffee each while Mrs. T had a glass of water. Then, while Tad paid the bill, Zeke escorted his Gram to the ladies room. He watched them walk away, feeling something like happiness settle in his chest. This was what a family breakfast should be like...sharing food, lots of laughter, and quiet conversation. It should feel like belonging, like home. Family breakfasts at the Meredith estate were never the warm cocoon in which he had been wrapped for the last hour. They had been interrogations—Zeke had experienced those—or strategy sessions, or else they'd been silent. He had learned to prefer the silence to the other two choices. But he could come to enjoy conversation with his morning coffee and eggs.

Mrs. T decided she preferred to walk only to the nearest gift shop where she pottered around looking for souvenirs, insisting Tad and Zeke go for a walk without her.

"I'll just wait for you on the lovely bench outside the shop. I'll be fine...I have Punkin with me."

And when Zeke looked ready to protest, she cut him off. "Now don't argue with your ole granny, boy.

176

Go ahead and spend a little time with Tad. I'll be underfoot the whole rest of the day."

She winked at Tad as she said it, giggling like a schoolgirl and getting a laugh from him for her troubles. She was the world's worst matchmaker, but he loved having her in his corner. He stepped away, giving Zeke the eye, and grinning when he shook his head and followed him.

"We won't be long, Gram," he promised her.

"Don't rush on my account," she told him. "I'm as happy as a pig in mud."

Tad knew exactly where he wanted to go. There was a long stretch of empty beach on the other side of the diner, away from the boardwalk. It was much less crowded, and he might be able to steal the kiss he had been wanting since he had seen Zeke pulling his shirt over his head in his doorway earlier. Now that he had tasted him, he was becoming addicted. But even if he couldn't get what he really wanted, at least he'd be alone with him for a little while before they'd have to go home where they'd be sharing space with his grandmother.

"Sorry about my Gram," Zeke said ruefully as they turned toward the beach. "She thinks she's some kind of matchmaker. She doesn't mean any harm, even if she does embarrassing things, like try to set me up."

"Cut her some slack," Tad said, echoing Zeke's words from the day before. "She loves you." He waggled his brows at Zeke before adding, "Besides, it can't be all that bad if *I'm* the one she's trying to set you up with. I mean, I'm all on board with that."

Zeke burst into amused laughter. "You're crazy."

"Maybe, but you like that about me. Go on, admit it."

They reached the beach and Tad headed them toward the empty side. "Maybe we can come back and go for a swim next time."

"Next time?"

"Yeah. Just you and me. Another date. Or maybe we can take this to my beach house instead. We can stay longer."

"You forget I'm a working man. I can't just up and leave."

"Neither can I," Tad replied. "But if we plan for it, we can do it. I'd like to do that with you."

"We'll see. Not making any promises. I still have to find a new job, remember?'

They were leaving the crowded section of beach behind, and the endless waves and sand stretched ahead of them.

"Are you looking for another private nursing gig?"

Tad wouldn't admit it, but he didn't want Zeke to find another job that put him in as close proximity with anyone else as he had been with him. They were still just getting to know each other, and he didn't want anyone else distracting him. But he had no right to try and dictate to Zeke how he lived his life and which jobs he chose to take on.

"I hadn't really been looking for a private nurse job when I landed yours," Zeke said, surprising him.

"So how did you end up with me?"

"I put my name in with an agency. To be honest, I was kind of shocked when I got a call asking

178

me to work with you. In my experience, rich folk don't choose people like me because they don't usually look in the places where I'm registered. There's a whole other network for the rich and famous."

Zeke spoke matter-of-factly, as though the bias he was describing was par for the course. If Tad hadn't been sick, he would never have known this kind of thing existed. And he would never have met Zeke. He didn't really know how his mother had found Zeke, and maybe he'd ask her, but frankly, he was just glad they'd met, and he said so.

"We were meant to meet," he replied. "Fate, kismet, God...whatever you believe in led us to each other. It was meant to be. Serendipity."

He stopped walking and turned to Zeke, needing him to see how serious he was. He held Zeke's gaze, not knowing how he would take his words. He leaned in and pressed his lips tentatively against Zeke's, unsure of his response, and sighed into his mouth when Zeke opened for him, deepening the kiss for a brief moment before pulling his mouth away. And then he surprised Tad by almost immediately agreeing with his comment.

"I agree. I believe everything happens when it's supposed to, and everything happens for a reason. I lost my job at the senior care facility because I was meant to care for you. So, I'm not gonna worry too much about where the next job will come from. I know it'll come when it's time."

He stopped, and Tad watched as he bent down and picked up a pretty shell, cleaning the sand from it and turning it over in his hand to examine it from all sides. He digested the words Zeke had just spoken, liking their profound simplicity. He knew he could never be quite so relaxed in his thinking, but Zeke's quiet acceptance was a calming force, making him believe anything was possible if he could just have faith. And he was more than ready to try.

Chapter Thirteen

September

"Are you comfortable, Mrs. T?"

Zeke watched as Tad fussed over his grandmother and bit back a smile. The two of them got on like a house on fire, and he couldn't stop smiling over it. After their walk, he had been as hungry for another kiss as he had seen in Tad's eyes, but they resisted. The hunger still burned inside him even now, a fire he didn't wish to quench. Instead of more kisses, they returned to find Gram seated comfortably on the bench outside the store shooting the breeze with a sprightly elderly gentleman who informed Zeke his grandmother was a pearl among women and if he were any younger and not on the brink of death, he'd sweep her off her feet and elope with her to Gretna Green.

The old guy was funny, but Zeke sensed somehow he wasn't joking. Would he be as cheerful if he knew he was dying? He didn't really know, but he did know that most people fought against dying tooth and nail. Zeke could imagine this guy planning a party for his memorial service instead of a traditional funeral. His spirit was warm and made Gram smile, for which Zeke was grateful. They'd left him when he assured them his granddaughters would take him home once they were finished in the store.

"Would you like anything else, Mrs. T?" Tad had asked and once she told him she had everything she needed, he'd taken them back to his condo.

He lived on the top floor of his apartment building and his penthouse, one of two on that level, overlooked the great park and the lake beyond it. The city was spread out below them, beautiful in the bright late summer sunshine. It was a spacious three-bedroom, three bathroom dwelling, luxurious and elegant. And yet, it looked like Tad with its dark, masculine decor, artwork and furnishings. Zeke liked the deep blues, the gold, chocolate tones, and the splashes of orange that warmed the space. Tad gave them the tour and then showed Gram where she could lie down when she was ready for a nap.

"Thank you, Tad," she said. "I'll be fine for now. But I would like to give Punkin some water, if you don't mind."

"Right this way."

Once the dog was set, Gram took up residence on the balcony, lying back on the lounger with a magazine from the stack Tad kept on the table out there. Zeke smiled as he observed her. He could tell she was contented, and it intensified the feelings for Tad he was grappling with.

"Your Gram is a brave lady." Tad's voice and his breath in his ear raised goosebumps on Zeke's skin. He shivered. He hadn't heard him move to stand behind him, in his personal space.

"Why do you say that?"

"I've had more than one party here, sometimes involving folks sleeping over, and half of them refuse to even go out there, never mind sit on the balcony, and they're half her age. We're pretty high up, but your Gram doesn't seem to be worried by that."

Admiration and respect dripped from his tones and Zeke's heart swelled with pride. Gram was a tough old bird. He knew that better than anyone else, but he was glad Tad recognized it as well.

"Yeah, she's pretty fearless." He turned to smile at Tad. "And you seem to have touched the soft spot inside her as well. Very few people ever do. Makes you pretty special, you know?"

He glanced over to where his grandmother sat, checking to see if she could see them from where she sat. The French doors were open and a cool breeze wafted in. Tad inhaled, and Zeke felt it down to his toes.

"I'm glad she likes me."

His words, breathed into Zeke's ears, sent more shivers racing through his system. "Me too."

He turned his head again to look at Tad and their lips met. For the briefest of moments, they stared into each other's eyes, and then Tad was turning him and they were devouring each other. Zeke couldn't think about what Gram might see if she chanced to glance their way. It wasn't as important as how Tad's kiss was making him feel. Hunger roared to life inside him, spreading liquid heat in his veins. His body was warming up as fast as his cock was plumping in his jeans. He shuddered when Tad wrapped his arms around him and pulled him closer.

And then their cocks were straining against each other, the heat between their bodies making Zeke's knees weak. He stumbled, and Tad held him and pulled him out of the line of sight of his grandmother. They held each other tightly, returning to nip at each other's lips as they strained their bodies together, wanting more than they knew they could have in that moment.

"Baby, we have to stop."

Zeke groaned when Tad dragged his mouth away, keeping his eyes closed as though that would

184

help him preserve the sweetness of the moment. He didn't want to stop kissing Tad. *Just one more kiss.* He loved the endearment Tad let slip. It made him feel treasured, needed, desired. *Call me "baby" again.* He swallowed the words that sprang to his lips and nodded, stepping away from Tad. His legs trembled enough that he had to steady himself with a hand on the wall next to him before he could move to sit at the kitchen counter. Tad moved away to the refrigerator and opened it, standing directly in front of it. Yeah, it wasn't just him that was hot. Tad obviously needed help cooling down as well, despite the air conditioning.

They had to ease the sexual tension between them quickly. It was all well and good for Gram to like Tad and to approve of whatever was happening between them. It was a whole other thing for her to witness the evidence of their passion for each other. Zeke didn't need her noticing the bulge in his crotch or Tad's kiss-swollen lips. What they did with each other was still very new and private.

"What do you fancy for lunch?" Tad turned to look at him, the heat of their encounter still burning in his eyes.

You. I want you for lunch. Zeke kept expression neutral, not willing to give away any of his thoughts. If he was to regain control, he had to rein himself in.

"I'm good. Gram won't have much...a cup of soup and a few crackers will keep her until dinner time."

"I'll look about that now, then. Why don't you go and keep her company? I don't want her to feel alone."

Zeke nodded and stood up, pausing when Tad called his name.

"This isn't over. We're not done."

"I know." His response was a croak of sound, his skin tingling with awareness.

He left Tad in the kitchen and went to sit with Gram, who was lying back, her eyes closed. He wondered if she was asleep until she said,

"Your young man is very kind, Zeke."

He sat down as she opened her eyes. "How did you know I was here?"

"I bought you the cologne you're wearin', remember? It's very distinctive." She gave him a smug smile before adding, "Tad wears an expensive scent as well."

"You've been sniffing him, too?" Zeke asked teasingly. He didn't bother to deny that Tad was his "young man." It wouldn't have made a difference to her opinion and it would have been a lie to pretend otherwise. Gram didn't take kindly to lying.

"I've been doin' more than that," she informed him with a self-satisfied smirk.

Zeke nodded. "I know." He looked out over the vista below them. "You liked him right away, didn't you?" He looked back to find her staring at him.

"I did. Any man of his social standin' who takes time to visit the elderly, and to bring gifts with him, has an honest soul and a warm heart." She pointed at Zeke to emphasize her next remark. "Do you see any pets here? I don't see a trace of any, yet he brought a total stranger to his home and let me bring my dog. What's not to like?"

Zeke couldn't argue with her assessment. Tad was a generous and gracious human being.

"And the way he looks at you when he thinks no one is watching him? I've only ever seen that look in one other man's eyes."

Zeke stayed quiet, waiting for her to finish her thought. He wanted to know how Tad looked at him, and more, he wanted to know if he looked at Tad in the same way. They hadn't known each other a long time, but Zeke knew they were on the brink of something special.

"Your father, God rest his soul, looked at your mother like that the very first time he saw her." Gram held his gaze, and Zeke saw the shimmer of tears in her eyes before she smiled and added, "He told her he loved her a week after they met." She chuckled. "*I* told him he was crazy. I called him a fool, letting his head be turned by a pretty face and a baby-making body." She sighed, clasping and unclasping her hands. "It was like nobody was talking to him. He ignored me completely."

Gram had never really told him much about his parents. He only knew he had been loved and wanted. He liked knowing they had loved each other, and that his father, after whom he'd been named, had been a sensitive and romantic man. He was glad of that, because it meant he was fine as he was. He didn't need to change or become someone different.

"Zeke, I want you to promise me you won't fight against your feelings for Tad. I was wrong about your father. He wasn't a fool. He wasn't crazy. He went after the woman he wanted and didn't let a single soul talk him out of his dream. For as long as they were together, he was the happiest I had ever seen him. I want that for you, son."

"I won't fight it, Gram." He couldn't, even when he tried. He was barely managing to control it.

She smiled tenderly at him and closed her eyes again.

"Don't fall asleep. Tad's making you some soup," Zeke told her.

She smiled, eyes still closed. "A true gentleman...and a cook."

After lunch, while Gram took a nap, Tad invited Zeke to share the hot tub with him. Zeke didn't have his swim shorts, and there was no way he was going naked in a hot tub with Tad while his grandmother was anywhere close by. So, he was forced to borrow a pair off Tad, whose delight in seeing how snugly they fit on his thighs knew no bounds. Where they were loose on Tad's slim hips, they hugged Zeke's ass like a second skin.

"You sexy beast, you!" Tad exclaimed, once he got his breath back when Zeke walked out of the bathroom.

Zeke laughed. "No more than you, Popeye!" He eyed Tad's body in the skin-tight swim trunks he wore.

"Aerodynamics," Tad said airily, as though that explained his choice of swimwear.

"Mhm, yeah, whatever dude! Let's go. I want to be back in my own clothes before Gram wakes up."

Tad winked at him. "Next time, we'll be alone. Then you won't even need to wear one."

Zeke rolled his eyes, chuckling at Tad's smirk. The water, when he stepped into the tub, was screamingly hot for the first few minutes till he got used to it. Then he settled his back against the side and accepted the beer Tad handed him.

"Here's to the memories!" Tad clinked his bottle against Zeke's.

"To the memories!"

He was definitely making new ones, sweet ones with Tad. He was new to being in a relationship, and he hadn't even dated all that much, but he was sure Tad had more experience than he did. Why else was he so cool, calm, and collected, even when lust rode him hard? Was he always in control? Did he ever give it up?

"What's got you frowning like that?"

Tad's question, coming out of the blue, alerted him to the fact he was thinking too much. He was there to relax and enjoy himself, not to worry about how much or how little experience he had. Tad didn't seem to care, and if the few kisses they had shared so far had been any indication, he was holding his own.

"Zeke? What are you thinking about?"

This time the question sounded worried. Zeke answered quickly. "It's nothing, really."

"Nothing sure looks heavy, dude!" Tad shifted until he was sitting next to Zeke, and put a finger to his chin, turning his face so he could look into his eyes. "Tell me."

"Is this how you get witnesses to confess? By turning on the charm?"

Maybe he could avoid sharing his insecurities by deflecting. Suddenly, he felt like an idiot for thinking about his performance in what was still a fairly new friendship. A few hot kisses did not make a

189

relationship, even if that was what he wanted. And he didn't want Tad to feel obliged to make more of it than he needed or desired. What if all he wanted was a friend with benefits? That was a long-term relationship, even if it didn't go beyond sex. That wasn't what he wanted, but Tad was a man of the world. He might not see the need for more. And Zeke would not be the man to impose his needs on anyone else.

"Thanks for the compliment, but you're wasting your time. I still want to know why you're fretting. Is Mrs. T okay? I saw the two of you talking earnestly before lunch, so I didn't intrude."

This was the perfect distraction. If he shared what Gram had told him, he could steer clear of the conversation about himself and how he measured up.

"Gram's fine. She was talking about you."

"What about me?"

"She says you look at me like my dad used to look at my mom, the way he always looked at her from the first time he saw her."

"And how was that?"

It occurred to Zeke then Gram hadn't actually described how his dad looked at his mom. She'd just said Tad looked at him like that. And did he really want to tell Tad his grandmother thought he was in love with her grandson? Was that any less awkward of a conversation to have? Fuck! He hid his sigh by sipping his beer.

"She didn't say. Just that he loved my mom a lot." Well, at least that was the summary version of it.

"How did your parents die?"

The question was unexpected, and while it did take them even further afield from Tad's original question, it was not a subject Zeke liked to dwell on. There was no way to make their deaths any less painful and horrible than it must have been, even though he didn't remember it, and he didn't want or need Tad's pity. But he had never been one to quibble. Look how well that had turned out when he tried it a few moments before!

"They were killed when I was very young. I don't remember it." He paused, then made up his mind to answer the question before it was asked. "They were murdered."

Her didn't look at Tad when he stopped speaking. He sipped his beer and looked out at the sky. A jetliner was streaming by overhead, leaving a fluffy contrail behind it. He studied the ever loosening plume of vapor, wondering why he was feeling emotional about a subject he very rarely even thought about. He barely remembered his parents. He had been barely two-years old when they had been strangled and stabbed in their bed. They had died in each other's arms, as Gram told it. No one had disturbed their bodies, it seemed, and though no official motive for the killing had ever been given, Gram knew they had been murdered because their love was forbidden.

To hear her tell it, Zeke had been lucky he was staying with her that night. It was the anniversary of their marriage, and his dad wanted to spend some time alone with his wife. It was Gram who taught him everything happens for a reason. She helped him to understand his life had been spared for a purpose, he should be grateful for it, and not mourn his parents' death as just a terrible injustice.

Some gifts come wrapped in ugly brown paper, and smelling of the fish it carried. Be grateful for the gift. Don't worry about what it came in.

He could almost hear her repeating that mantra over and over to him, especially in the days after he was beaten up and almost killed, when the story of his parents' murder returned to haunt his dreams. He had needed counseling to help him past those nightmares. And now, here he was again, feeling the weight of his unhappy history.

"Zeke, come on. Let's go back in."

He looked up to find Tad standing outside the tub and offering him a towel. When had he gotten out? Shit! He'd gotten lost in his head again and spoiled their time alone.

"I'm sorry, Tad. I didn't mean to get all morose." He hurried to apologize for his lapse.

"Hey." Tad cupped his face. "Stop. It's okay."

He leaned in and pressed his lips against Zeke's. It was a comforting kiss, and Zeke wrapped his arms around him and hugged him, grateful for the support he hadn't known he needed until that moment.

"Thanks. Not sure why that happened…"

"Babe, it doesn't matter how old you were or how little you remember. They were still your parents. Somewhere in your subconscious, you feel the pain of their loss. I'm sure it's quite normal."

Tad sounded so reasonable Zeke took heart and relaxed. The swim shorts clung even more tenaciously to his frame, leaving nothing to the imagination. It was a good thing he was calm, though even he had to admit that hard or soft, his package was nothing to sneeze at. He wrapped the towel around his hips on

192

the off chance that Gram was awake. He'd rather not blind her with his over-abundant blessings. The thought made him chuckle, which made Tad look at him.

"Now what?"

"Nothing. Really!" he added hastily when Tad gave him a look. "I was just imagining Gram's reaction to seeing me in these wet swim shorts."

Tad's laughter filled the spaces inside him that the story of his parents had opened up. He inhaled deeply, needing to hold the warmth inside.

"You're right. We'd best hurry up and change."

While Gram napped, Tad made some calls in his office, and Zeke vegged out on the couch, watching reruns of a favorite cooking show. When Punkin barked, he turned his head and watched his grandmother walking slowly out to the living room, leaning heavily on her cane. The dog seemed to know not to run around her legs, because he walked sedately beside her, jumping up into her lap the moment she sat in the leather recliner.

"This New Zealand chef reminds me of that English woman I also like to watch. The buxom one with the dark hair, thick lips, and pretty smile."

Zeke knew who she meant. He liked her as well. "She's not on right now, Gram," he said. "Want me to change the channel?"

"No, no! I'll watch whatever you have going. But may I have a snack?"

"Like some fruit, maybe?" he asked, rising to his feet.

"Sounds good. What did you boys get up to while I was napping?"

Zeke turned back from where he was standing to look at his grandmother. Did she just sound like she was teasing him? What exactly did she think they had done? Did he even want to know? He looked into her eyes and decided that no, he didn't want to know.

Shaking his head in amusement, he said, "We spent a little time in the hot tub, and I told Tad what you said about him." Before she could ask why, he added, "He wanted to know what we were talking about so earnestly. I told him it was about him."

"And what did he think about that?"

Tad walked in at that moment, and Zeke hurried away, not wanting to hear his answer. They hadn't really talked about it, and he would rather not have that anxiety from earlier return to mess with the rest of the day. He pulled a banana, an apple, a peach, and an orange from the fruit bowl on the kitchen island and began to make a quick salad in a bowl he pulled from the dishwasher.

Tad walked in as he was assembling it, and asked, "Want some yogurt to dress that up a bit?"

"Sure. Gram wants a snack. I hope you don't mind..."

Tad came around to where he stood at the center island and took the spoon from his hand. Placing it in the bowl, he took Zeke's hands in his.

"I brought you here because I want you to know where I live. Because I expect to spend a lot of time here with you. So no, I don't mind. I don't care what you use or what you do, as long as you're comfortable. Relax."

He ended his little speech with a quick and dirty kiss that reverberated all the way down to Zeke's toes. Then he turned back to get the yogurt while Zeke swore mildly.

"Fuck!"

Tad reappeared before him, a smirk on his face. "Soon, I hope," he murmured, stealing another kiss from Zeke's lips before handing him individual containers of yogurt. "I didn't know which flavor she'd like best. That's all I have in the fridge."

Then he walked away nonchalantly as though he hadn't just set Zeke's cock on edge again. *Fucking cock tease!* And damn if he didn't love it!

Chapter Fourteen

September

By the time Tad dropped Mrs. T back home, he was so on edge he thought he would burst with need. She decided she preferred to take dinner with her back to the home so she could share it with her friends. While she called her friends to tell them her plan, Tad made her a nice care package, including chocolate and fruit for dessert, and they had seen her safely back to her room before dinner time. Now they were on their way to Zeke's place. It was still early—barely five in the afternoon—and he was glad of it since he needed to spend more than the fleeting moments of time he already had with Zeke.

So much ground had been covered today, and yet there were so many things left unsaid. They hadn't discussed what his grandmother had meant by comparing him to Zeke's dad. Did she mean he was in love with Zeke? He wouldn't deny it, even if he wasn't sure of it. He knew it was more than lust that he felt, though right now that was the most overpowering of the emotions churning in his gut. He didn't know whether they would get to the hot-as-fuck kisses they had shared already, but he would cross that bridge when he got to it. For now, he was just glad he would get to be with Zeke alone for a while before he had to return to his own empty apartment and the realities of his existence.

Maybe instead of stewing things over in his head, he should start the conversation they needed to have before they got to the stuff he couldn't get his mind off. At least conversation would help to ease the constriction in his jeans.

"So, what exactly did your grandmother tell you about your parents? We never managed to finish that conversation."

Zeke's sigh told him he didn't want to have this one, either, but there was no way he was backing down from this discussion. He was intrigued by the old woman's insight, and he loved that she didn't mind. How great would it have been to have had that kind of unquestioning acceptance when he was seventeen and coming out to his folks! He loved being embraced and treated with open, unquestioning affection.

"She said the first time my dad saw my mom he had a look on his face that he had for all the time they were together. And he told her he loved her after they'd known each other a week." He chuckled, and Tad glanced over at him, waiting for the rest. "She said she told him he was crazy to think he could love someone after only a week based on her face and her body. She told him he was a fool, but he ignored her."

"Guess your dad knew what he wanted, huh?"

"I guess. He was a romantic, a sensitive guy." Another pause, and then he added wistfully, "I wonder what he would have been like if he had lived? Would he be cool with me liking guys instead of girls, or would he have told me I'm crazy, too?"

Tad reached over and rested his hand on Zeke's thigh, squeezing it gently. "I'd like to think he'd be cool with you and love you just the way you are. The way your Gram loves you and accepts you, no questions asked. In fact, I'd like to think you're just like he would have been if he'd been allowed to live."

The feel of Zeke's hand on his squeezing in return, settled something in him that had been on edge all day. And it solidified the emotions that centered around Zeke, made them have a new weight and substance. Maybe Mrs. T was right. Maybe he was in love with her grandson.

"So, getting back to the question, she said I look at you the same way your dad looked at your mom, huh? That means she thinks I'm in love with you, right?"

Silence greeted his question, but he waited. He had been a good prosecutor precisely because he had the patience of Job when he needed it. He turned his hand under Zeke's, palm up, and clasped their fingers together.

"I think that's what she thinks, yes."

Finally, an answer, and from the sound of it, an honest one. He loved that Zeke didn't try to hide behind lies, though he had tried an evasion earlier. Maybe Zeke wasn't ready to talk about love yet. Tad could understand that. He spent all his time in the Navy, and the last two years out of it, avoiding even thinking about relationships that were not about sex alone. And even those connections were fleeting to protect himself from the possibility of discovery. So even if he was finally ready to step out of the closet he had allowed himself to settle in, there were still hurdles to overcome...like helping his younger lover—soon, please God!—to accept that what he was feeling was actually love.

"Do you think she's wrong? Or are you scared she may be right?"

Their hands remained clasped, for which Tad was grateful. He liked the connection while they talked. And it meant, even if Zeke was a little bit terrified of what was happening, he wasn't against it.

"I'm worried more than scared." Tad could hear the diffidence in his tone as he made his admission.

"Why?" Tad couldn't imagine what would worry a self-confident man like Zeke.

"I'm a grown man with zero experience of relationships. I don't like to fail. It's not in my DNA, according to Gram. But even she can't know how I'll do in this."

How did he answer Zeke? What could he say, a man who had hidden from the world for most of his life? He could only be honest. That was all he had, at the end of the day.

"I don't have any experience with long term relationships either, Zeke. The most I've had have been some hookups to scratch an itch."

Was he really going to do this? Was he going to finally confess his cowardice to someone he had only known a few months? Even if it were someone he cared about? What if Zeke lost interest? What would he gain by telling the truth now? What would he lose?

Inhaling deeply to crank up his resolve, he continued, "No one in the Navy knew for sure what my sexual orientation was. I couldn't take the chance because of what happened to my best friend while I was in the Academy."

They had reached Zeke's subdivision by this time, and he wasn't sure he could talk about it and drive. So, he squeezed Zeke's hand again and got them onto his driveway. Then he switched off the engine and turned to face him.

"His name is Ben and he's gay. He couldn't tell his parents...they wouldn't have understood and would have tried to change him. He enlisted in the

Army, graduated from boot camp, and was on leave before his first deployment. And he was almost killed before his first deployment. He never left the States. They found him in the hotel room where he had gone to be with a guy he met for sex. He was so badly beaten, it took him a year just to get back to full mobility."

Pain welled up inside him at the thought of his friend. Ben didn't recognize him anymore. He was lost inside his head, the trauma of his beating, and the knowledge of why it had happened had broken his teenage mind.

"Is he still alive?"

Tad's gentle question softened the hard knot of rage that was building inside him. He swallowed.

"Yeah...in a facility in Florida. It's not run by the military but there are a number of patients there who are former military. I send money for his care, because his parents disowned him."

They were still holding hands, and Tad felt Zeke's own tighten in his. Finally, someone he could share this burden of knowledge with. Someone who understood. Someone who cared. He took a breath and went on.

"*Don't Ask, Don't Tell* was never a guarantee of safety for LGBTQ people in the military, and I was young enough to be scared I'd never make it out alive, either. In those days, I was prepared to die at sea, but not because I'm bisexual."

"Did you try with women?" Zeke's voice held gentle inquiry.

"Once in a while, a woman looked interesting, but nothing ever came of it. And I never relaxed enough to check out the men except fleetingly, when I was sure no one would see. But I didn't try most times, and the few hookups I managed were half and half."

Zeke reached over and hugged him with the arm that was free. "I'm so sorry, Tad."

He pushed out a heavy breath. "I only told you so you'd know we're sort of in the same boat. Anything we do, we're learning it together. Sure, I've had more hookup experience than you, but they don't teach you how to romance a guy, or how to win him when you find him."

"Damn! Where did you learn the sweet talking, then?"

Tad chuckled, the pain easing and the passion resurfacing. "It comes naturally, I guess. I make my living using words." He leaned in and buzzed Zeke's lips. "So, may I come in and practice my romancing skills?"

"Yeah. Let's go inside. I'd rather not give my neighbors an eyeful."

He reached behind him for the basket with the care package Tad had packed for them so they could have dinner, and they went in together. Punkin was antsy, so Zeke took him for a walk, and by the time he got back, Tad warmed the meal and set the dining table for two. He'd found two candles and wine glasses and hunted around till he found matching cutlery. He added some gold linen napkins to the dark green tablecloth already on the oval table, and tuned his phone to one of the channels that played slow jams.

When Zeke returned to feed the dog, he said, "Dinner's in the dining room as soon as you've washed up."

When Zeke walked in, Tad lit the candles and held his chair out for him, kissing him sweetly on the lips before allowing him to sit down.

"Dig in," he said when he took his own seat.

"Don't mind if I do. This smells delicious."

Tad smiled, knowing Zeke would enjoy the steak and twice-baked stuffed potatoes with a green salad. They ate in silence, except for Zeke's moans of pleasure at the food and Tad's quiet chuckles in response. Truth be told, he barely noticed what he ate, because he was in such a hurry to get to the best part...the part where he got to taste the man having a *foodgasm* over his dinner. He poured them both a second glass of wine, emptying the bottle, and once Zeke was done eating, he cleared away the dishes, packing them in the dishwasher and wiping down the counters.

"Where do I put the soiled napkins?" he asked, returning to the dining room where Zeke was blowing out the candles.

"I'll take that. Go sit. You've done enough."

"Let me take your wine."

Tad took his glass and walked into the pretty living room, where he placed both glasses on the coffee table on coasters conveniently left there for the purpose. Then he settled into the loveseat and beckoned Zeke over when he walked in.

"Come sit next to me." He smiled, knowing it was probably predatory and not caring.

Zeke lifted a brow and chuckled, but he went and sat next to Tad. "Little snug, isn't it?"

Tad grinned. "I like snug. Easier access to...everything."

Zeke laughed. "You're hilarious, you know that?"

Tad shrugged. "I'm honest. And I need to kiss you. You got a problem with that?"

"Only if you don't shut up and kiss me now." Zeke turned his body so he was facing Tad and leaned in, not taking his eyes off him as Tad met him halfway.

Zeke's lips were warm and a little dry. The feel of them against his own stirred Tad's blood impossibly. No way in hell was he going to be able to avoid becoming addicted to the taste and the scent of the man he held in his arms. Zeke tasted of the wine he'd been drinking, and of sweetness and something spicy and elemental that Tad knew was all Zeke. He licked the dry lips beneath his own and Zeke opened them with a groan of pleasure, spiking Tad's desire up another notch.

"You like that, babe?"

Tad's breath was coming in hard pants as he strove to keep calm. He lifted his mouth away from the pillowy lips beneath it, waiting for Zeke to answer, giving himself a moment to regain some measure of control.

"You know I do."

Zeke's voice was raw with emotion. Tad had never heard this tone from him before. It was needy, hungry, aching for something only Tad could give him.

"Should I make you wait before I taste you again?" he wondered aloud, ghosting his breath over Zeke's lips without touching them. "I feel like you need to get a taste of your own medicine, know what it's like to want the thing you're being denied from the only one you want it from."

Zeke chuckled and nipped his lips, making Tad moan in delight and anticipation. "Yeah, you could do that," he conceded, licking the places he had just nipped with barely-there swipes of his tongue. "But that would mean denying yourself as well, wouldn't it?" He paused, pulling away to look into Tad's eyes, darkened to a stormy gray. "Are you prepared to suffer with me?"

He bussed Tad's lips quickly and pulled away again, smiling with so much warm affection Tad knew he was lost. Although he had been the one to initiate this new level of intimacy in their relationship, it was clear Zeke was in control. Anything he wanted, Tad would give him. And all they'd done was kiss each other. He supposed in another life he would have hated that, but here, at this moment, he couldn't muster even one iota of outrage. He loved to see this side of Zeke. It turned him on even more, making his body harden desperately.

"It won't be suffering if it's with you," Tad whispered against his lips before opening his mouth over Zeke's again, taking the kiss they both wanted, sending both their pulses soaring.

Zeke opened to him, pulling him into his wider body, wrapping his beefy arms around Tad, enveloping him in a fiery cocoon of need and lust and...dare he think love? He couldn't speak for Zeke, but he knew what he was feeling for the younger man was love. It had been forever ago since he had felt

204

anything like the emotions sweeping through him as he devoured Zeke's mouth, trying desperately to satisfy his thirst for him.

"I never would have pegged you for a kisser," Zeke said, pulling his mouth away to tease Tad's cheeks and the skin behind his earlobes. "You always seemed to be ready for the next step, always in a hurry, never one to waste time on things like foreplay."

Tad pouted. "Such a poor perception you have of me," he groused, nipping Zeke's earlobe as he passed by on his way down to his throat. "I'm not always in a hurry."

"Maybe not, but you aren't always patient, either. You seemed like a kid at Christmas. I bet you couldn't wait to unwrap your presents."

Tad chuckled even as he reached for Zeke's shirt, pulling it from his pants and beginning to unbutton it.

"You would win that bet hands down," he admitted, pulling another button free and reveling in the expanse of chest being revealed to his hungry eyes.

The sight of Zeke's body always made his own hum with need, and now, hungry as he was for more and finally having Zeke's consent, he was hard-pressed to hold back the moan of delight at being able at last to touch all the places he had longed for before..."hard" being the operative word. He finished unbuttoning the shirt and drew it slowly down Zeke's arms, humming the stripper song as he did so, making his soon-to-be-lover chuckle.

"Shouldn't that be Christmas music?" Zeke asked.

Tad grinned. "All I want for Christmas is you," he sang softly in Zeke's ear, wondering at how relaxed he felt with him, and marveling at the laughter blossoming between them.

He'd never seduced anyone with humor before, but it was a fucking turn-on to hear Zeke's deep chuckle. Maybe Zeke was right to say he was an immediate gratification kind of guy. And maybe this slow-burn buildup of desire was worth giving up that particular predilection. He leaned in and kissed Zeke's right nipple, letting his tongue linger over its hardening, pebbled surface. Zeke's groan of appreciation was reward enough for his effort to slow down, and the sound of that rumble of pleasure slid down to his balls, tightening them and hardening his dick.

"You sure you haven't been with anyone recently?"

Zeke's question made Tad pause. He looked him in the eye, trying to read the expression in them. "That's a dash of cold water right there. Why do you ask?"

Zeke inhaled sharply. "Because you're driving me crazy. So, either you've been practicing, or I'm a lightweight greenhorn."

Tad kept his gaze on Zeke's face. He had to ask the question because, despite his confession about never having been in a relationship, it hadn't occurred to him Zeke meant he had never been with anyone *at all*.

"What are you saying, babe?"

Now it was Zeke's turn to study his face. Tad waited quietly, knowing he would hear only the truth when Zeke answered him.

"You really want me to say it out loud?"

His discomfort was palpable. Tad could almost imagine the thoughts racing through his head, and he didn't want the man he was growing fonder of every day to have even a moment's disquiet. But he needed to hear the words. He wouldn't assume any longer.

"Yeah, I need you to tell me. It won't make a difference to me, but I don't want to assume anything."

Color washed up Zeke's cheeks, and he lowered his eyes for a moment before seeming to gather himself and raising them to Tad's own.

"You'll be my first," he said, almost abashed, and lowered his eyes again.

Time paused, the moment swirling around them in slow motion, every beat of Zeke's heart reverberating against the palm of Tad's hand as he spread his fingers over Zeke's chest. His own heartbeat matched the rhythm of the one under his hand, anticipation and lust speeding them both.

"Fuck, Zeke!"

Tad couldn't think of anything else to say. Maybe once the lust riding his ass abated, he'd be more coherent, but for now, his hand trembled as he stripped the shirt off Zeke's hard body and threw it aside. This would be the best gift he had ever received, and he was going to make sure Zeke enjoyed everything he had ever learned about how to please a lover.

"Look at me," he asked gently, needing to see more of Zeke. "Let me see your eyes, babe."

He resisted the urge to pull his chin up. He wanted Zeke to submit to their mutual desire, beginning with maintaining eye contact. Everything they would do would be infinitely more intimate if they looked each other in the eye as they did it. Tad wanted that level of intimacy with Zeke, even more than he wanted to fuck him raw. It shocked him how much he wanted to be intimate with Zeke, to know him on a cellular level, beyond the fireworks of lovemaking. He had never wanted anything like this in all his life, and now that he did, he would search it out and nurture it and fight to keep it until the day he died.

When Zeke raised his eyes to Tad's, the hunger in their depths shook him to the very core of his being. He'd never seen such need directed at him before. It blazed out at him, pure and unfettered. He could almost hear Zeke asking for...what? What did this man he wanted need from him?

"What is it, love?" he asked. "What can I do for you? What do you need from me?"

He caressed Zeke's face as he waited, his thumbs stroking down the curve of his cheeks, tracing the scar on his left cheekbone down to the corner of his mouth, finding the divot in his chin and leaning in to lick it.

"Tell me," he breathed against Zeke's lips before licking each in turn, and peppering his face with butterfly kisses.

"Kiss me." Zeke swallowed, the sound of his anxiety making Tad smile.

"Like this?" Tad rubbed his nose against Zeke's inhaling him, loving the scent of man that hit him like a fast-moving train. "Or maybe like this?" He bussed his cheeks and his lips tenderly, alighting and flitting away before Zeke's tongue would catch him.

"Like this."

Zeke reached up, holding his head steady and pressing his mouth against Tad's, sending his tongue out to sip at Tad's lips before settling in the seam, demanding and expecting entry. Tad opened for him, and they kissed each other with everything they were feeling settling between and inside them. Tad's need rose like a wave, forcing him to drag his mouth away so he could grasp at life-giving air. Then he dove in again, riding the building tide of lust that saw them frantically undressing each other on the way to Zeke's bedroom where they fell in a tangled heap of trembling limbs on his wide bed.

Harsh breaths salted the heated air of the bedroom, the growing darkness ignored in favor of their desperate craving for more of each other. Tad nipped Zeke's lips sharply, soothing the ache with his heavy tongue, licking and sucking his lover into his mouth before moving inexorably down his big body, tasting and savoring him, driving them both wild.

"Do you have any idea how long I've wanted to get you here?"

Zeke shook his head and leaned in for another kiss. "No."

"Since maybe the day you moved into my family's house. I looked at you in that room unpacking, and all I could see was your legs hanging off the bed, with me between them, making you howl for me."

"So, what's stopping you now?" Zeke's question was a passionate growl.

The breathless challenge was all the permission Tad needed. "Fuck! I'll make you feel so good, babe."

He meant it. He would make this a night to remember for the man he was falling for. Mrs. T was right...he was in love with Zeke, and he would do everything he knew to do to show him how much he cherished him, how much he valued his place in his life. Starting now.

Chapter Fifteen

September

Tad's hands cupping Zeke's face as he kissed him were a warm and trembling testament to the heated desire that pulsed between them. He licked Zeke's lips and suckled his tongue before moving down to explore his neck and collarbones. Zeke shuddered with the urgency of his need. He had fooled around enough to know what lust felt like, and his urgent self-help showed him how it could be, but nothing had prepared him for the total ownership of his body Tad seemed bent on pursuing. No surface was free from Tad's tongue and lips and fingers. Zeke discovered he seemed to have more erogenous zones than a centipede had legs and every brush of Tad's mouth and hands against them brought him ever closer to an edge he had never been over before.

"Fuck, Tad, please!"

Was he only begging to be fucked? He didn't really know. All he knew for sure was he wanted more of the touches that cherished even as they owned him. And he wanted to reciprocate, but Tad wouldn't let him move. He groaned as Tad inhaled deeply at his groin, where his leg met his torso.

"You smell so damn good, baby. I could just eat you up!" Tad's growl was hoarse and hungry.

Zeke could only moan in acknowledgement of the compliment, as he was too busy losing his mind to the stroke of Tad's hand on his cock. And soon the moans morphed into whimpers as Tad settled one hand to caressing his balls and the other to stroking and twisting his cock. Then he watched as Tad lowered his head and licked the head of his straining dick. Fire shot up his spine and he moaned louder.

"Fuck, Tad!"

"Soon, baby. Be patient, okay? Good things come to those who wait."

Tad's playful wink turned him on even as it pissed him off. Why the hell was he teasing him so unmercifully? And why the fuck should he wait? He gasped when Tad took his cock head into his mouth and sucked on it, like it was a lollipop.

"Shit! That feels so fucking good, Tad!" He was going to die. Tad was going to kill him with pleasure. "Oh, fuck! Right there! Just like that!"

Tad chuckled, obviously delighted with his response. "Your wish is my command, babe."

And then he did it again, sliding his hand around the hard shaft while teasing that sweet spot just below his cock head. He was going to spontaneously combust...what? Oh shit! Tad's finger, wet with his precum, slid across his hole. He tightened it reflexively.

"Relax, baby. Gonna make you feel even better now."

Tad slid up his belly to lay another dirty kiss on his mouth, and he tasted himself on Tad's tongue. When had he ever tasted as good as he did in Tad's mouth? He had tasted his own cum before, but it had never turned him on the way even the faint traces of it on Tad's tongue wound him up. His thoughts were a jumble of desire, pleasure and thrilling anticipation as Tad circled his hole before pushing the tip of his finger in. He held his breath, but Tad was having none of it.

"Breathe for me, Zeke. Deep breaths, baby. Yeah, just like that. Now when I tell you, breathe out and push like you're constipated. Ready?"

Zeke nodded, eager to please his lover, eager to feel the next pleasure on this menu of carnal delights.

"Now, baby. Push out now."

Zeke did as he was told and felt Tad's finger slide into his hole. It burned for a moment but he bore it, knowing instinctively that the pleasure would come.

"More," he begged. "Please, give me more!"

Tad's finger pushed in and Zeke groaned. It felt so strange having anything inside him, strange and so intimate. Tad pushed all the way in and then withdrew almost the whole way out.

"Don't stop!" His demand was harsh, all he could manage while his mind and body reeled with sensation as Tad finger fucked him.

"I wouldn't dream of it," Tad murmured, sending a second finger up to join the first.

The burn returned for a moment, and Zeke had enough presence of mind to wonder how he was going to take anything as large as a cock up there, and then he forgot to think as Tad curled his finger and touched a magic button inside him.

Zeke screamed. Then he panted like a woman in labor as Tad did it again and again. He couldn't catch his breath, and precum streamed freely from his slit.

"God, I'm gonna cum, Tad! Oh fuck, I'm gonna cum!"

He growled when Tad immediately removed his fingers. What the hell was he playing?

"Condoms? Lube?" Tad had to repeat the question because he barely heard him.

"Side table, bottom drawer."

214

He pointed in the general direction, feeling all his limbs too weak to move. He watched Tad sheathe himself and slick lube all over that huge dick, and then he slid three lubed fingers back into Zeke's ass, pumping in and out roughly, hitting that magical button.

"Tad!" He screamed his name as cum boiled in his sacs.

"Don't you fucking cum till I'm inside you, you hear me?" When Zeke nodded his understanding, Tad growled again. "Roll over! Get on your hands and knees."

He looked up at him curiously. "Why?"

"Don't wanna hurt you. It'll be easier this way for your first time."

Tad was panting lightly now, which Zeke took as a good sign. He wasn't the only one coming undone. He positioned himself the way Tad wanted, and whimpered when Tad reached between his legs to caress his hanging sac again and to stroke his cock before positioning his cock at his hole.

"I'll go real slow, Zeke, I promise. Don't wanna hurt you."

Zeke tensed when the big head of Tad's thick erection pushed against his virgin hole.

"Relax, babe. Remember what I told you to do?" Zeke nodded. "Do that as I push in. It'll burn for a few, but then it'll get real good fast. I promise."

Zeke pushed against him as he pushed in and when Tad was seated to the root, his balls resting against the globes of Zeke's ass, nothing had ever felt that good to him. Tad stayed still until the burning stopped.

"Ready?" he asked finally.

"Yes! Fuck me, Tad!"

Slow even strokes gave way to faster, more frenzied rutting until neither man could halt the raging torrent of lust that swept them along in its path. Tad filled him over and over with his dick, adjusting his angle until Zeke's howl of delight told him he'd hit pay dirt. Then he kept hitting that spot, and soon Zeke was literally seeing stars as his orgasm built. He reached out a hand to jerk himself, needing to cum, but Tad smacked his hand away.

"Don't need that this time. Wanna make you cum without touching yourself. Wanna drive you insane so you can't help but blow. Wanna show you how good it can be with the right man. Wanna show you that man is me. Take me, baby. Take all of me."

Zeke pushed back against the invading rod and Tad groaned his pleasure. "Yeah, that's right, fuck me. Take every fucking drop of pleasure you need from me."

Zeke turned his head to look at his lover, and Tad kissed him on the mouth, shoving his tongue in like a mini cock. Zeke broke, screaming out his orgasm into Tad's mouth, losing himself to the waves of pleasure that rolled over him. His cock spurted ropes of cum, painting the sheets beneath him. He kept pushing back against Tad's cock, feeling it spurt as Tad swore with the strength of his own release. He took the ramming Tad didn't seem able to ease until there was nothing left to give. Tad's hips slowed, and Zeke sank to the bed, utterly spent.

"Don't fall asleep in the wet spot, baby."

Tad's voice reached Zeke from far away. "Go away. Too tired to move."

Tad chuckled. How did he have the energy to do that after that monster orgasm?

"Come here, Sleepy!" He pulled Zeke into his arms away from the cum-soaked spot on his sheets. "Sleep now. I've got you."

They made love twice more that night, and Tad ended up leaving in the wee hours of the morning.

"I have to go in to work these days," he quipped as he pushed his wrinkled shirt into his jeans. "Call you later?"

"You better."

"Come here." Tad opened his arms and Zeke walked into them, wrapping his own around Tad's smaller frame. "I had a great time yesterday, and last night was the best of all." He leaned his head back so he could look Zeke in the eye. "Thank you."

Zeke wrinkled his brows in confusion. If anything, he should be thanking Tad for making his first time so memorable...just like he said he would. "What for?"

"For choosing me to be your first."

Zeke could feel himself blushing, but he spoke his own gratitude anyway. "Thanks for making it worth the wait." He leaned in and kissed his lover. "You'd better go. You don't want to be late your first full day back without a nurse in tow."

"Happy job hunting." Another lazy kiss and then Tad opened the door and stepped out into the chilly pre-dawn.

"Thanks. Drive safely."

He couldn't settle down once Tad left. He went for his morning run, took Punkin out, fed him and then

217

showered and stood in the kitchen in his boxers drinking coffee. His ass was sore, but he didn't care. It was his reminder there was actually someone out there who was his. And even though he knew there was a lot to be done, he savored the sweetness of that knowledge. Eventually, he sat in front of his laptop and updated his resume before resubmitting it to the service he already uploaded it to. Then he researched other job placement sites and submitted it to two more before calling it a day.

He wasn't used to being idle, but the house didn't need cleaning, he had no dirty laundry, aside from his sweat-and-cum-soaked sheets, and he had done the grocery shopping. It wasn't time to make dinner as yet, and he couldn't think of anything else to do. He might as well finish the sweater he'd been knitting and maybe get a head start on the next blanket. He'd have to call to see when he could visit the children's ward next.

His cellphone ringing woke him up and he looked around wildly, still half asleep until he saw it. Grabbing it quickly, he answered without looking at the caller ID.

"Hello!"

"Is it me, or are you as exhausted as fuck?"

Zeke laughed. "You just woke me up from a nap, so I'm pretty sure it's not just you. Aside from being tired, how's your day going?"

"More of the same...one boring meeting after another, tons of reading and writing."

"Any headaches?"

"No. Nurse Taylor. I'm fine."

Tad's teasing tone made Zeke chuckle. "Don't get sassy with me. Someone has to look after you."

"Well, then, I'm glad it's you, babe."

Tad's voice softened and Zeke loved it as much as he loved the other variations. He wanted him there, now, so he could cuddle with him and take care of him.

"How much longer will you be at work?"

"I don't know. I have an evening meeting at six, and it may end up being a dinner meeting. I'll let you know. Want me to drop by before I go home?"

"I don't want to add to your stress, Tad."

"Is that a yes? Sounds like a 'yes' to me, so I'll see you later, then."

That became the pattern of the next few evenings. Sometimes they ended with Tad in Zeke's bed, asleep and worn out. Other times, they cuddled and then he went home. September was drawing to a close, the days growing cooler, the nights longer, and their feelings deeper. Zeke knew he was in love with Tad, but he wanted the time to be just right to tell him so. He didn't want to rush it, just in case. Then Tad told him he had a business trip coming up, the first since they had gotten together. Zeke's heart stuttered.

"How long will you be gone?"

He had known that trips were part of Tad's job description. Hell, the last thing Tad remembered had been the business trip he'd been about to go on a month before his accident. So why the hell was this throwing him for a loop? He felt an almost breathless panic, but he hid it, determined not to let Tad see how affected he was by the news.

"Depends on how long it takes my clients to decide what they want to do about the contract. It could be as few as two days or as many as weeks."

Not the most reassuring response and definitely not what he wanted to hear. What was he supposed to do while Tad went running off to some foreign country for work? *Get a fucking grip, that's what, Taylor!* He spoke sternly to himself. *If you got another private nursing gig that required you to live in, you'd do what had to be done because it's your job. Calm the fuck down!*

"When are you leaving? And where are you going?" He managed to keep his voice steady.

"The day after tomorrow to Geneva. May I come by tomorrow night?"

"You know you don't need to ask," Zeke said, kissed him, needing to drown his fear in lovemaking.

"I'd like to spend the whole night with you, babe."

"What time's your flight?" He would never refuse Tad.

"Eight, so I'll need to leave at five to make it to the airport in time."

"I'll make you breakfast to go." Because that's what you did when you cared for someone.

When Tad came over the next night after work carrying his luggage, Zeke tamped down the urge to grab him and kiss the shit out of him before he even set foot in the house. He had some news of his own, anyway. Tad brought his go bag and a suit in with him, and Zeke let him pass before turning to close the door and push him up against it.

"I've been needing to do this since you called to say you were on the way," he told him, and planted an electrifying kiss on Tad's equally hungry lips.

"I thought I was the impatient one," Tad said with a laugh when he dragged his lips away from Zeke's. "Instead, I've created a monster, it seems."

Zeke shut him up by the simple expedient of introducing his tongue into Tad's mouth again, sucking on it like a babe at the breast. He was pleased Tad took the hint and kept kissing him instead of trying to talk more. Talking could wait. He'd be without his lover for God only knew how long, and he wasn't ready to face that separation. Tad must have felt the desperation in his kiss because he pulled away again to cup Zeke's face in his hands.

"What's wrong, Zeke? You're so...intense tonight? What happened today?"

"Nothing happened. I got a call for a job interview, that's all. Actually, based on the conversation I had with the client, I'll get the job, but they want to meet me in person just to make sure I'm not an axe murderer or something equally sinister," he said, forcing a chuckle. Best start with the good news and try to keep things light. As he expected, Tad was delighted for him.

"Well, that's great news, isn't it? You'll be in a new position by the time I get back."

"If they like my face, yeah. It's another rehab position, but not live-in. The old lady fell and broke a bunch of bones, including her hip. She lives with her daughter, who is a working mom with a small child. I'll be there before the daughter leaves until she gets back home from work."

Tad leaned in again and kissed him softly. "Congratulations, love! You're gonna blow them away with how well you take care of your patient."

"Thanks. Come on. I made us dinner." Zeke turned away, taking the suit and Tad's bag into the bedroom. "I'll just go get things warm while you wash up."

He escaped to the kitchen, feeling like he dodged a bullet. Maybe Tad would think he was just preoccupied and he wouldn't have to answer any more questions. He wanted to forget his sadness and lose himself in his lover's arms before five in the morning. Earlier, since Tad had to shower and dress. He pulled the lasagna from the oven and laid the table. Tad walked back in as he was pulling two beers from the refrigerator.

"Have a seat. I hope I did this right. Gram gave me the recipe and instructions. She talked me through it."

He was proud of himself. He wasn't an accomplished cook like Tad, who did it to relax. But he wanted to learn, especially since he'd be living on his own. He had a suspicion his grandmother would choose to remain where she was currently residing, which left him the house all to himself. He hoped the dish would taste okay.

"Well, come on, then, Let's get to eating. I can't wait to taste this."

"Help yourself," Zeke invited him, and served himself from the salad bowl while Tad tackled the lasagna. Then they switched and before long Tad was making noises of delight.

"This is delicious, babe." He took another forkful into his mouth and chewed appreciatively, then licked his lips and added, "You follow directions very well. That's good to know."

Zeke looked up and caught the gleam of something in Tad's eyes. Were they still talking about food? Tad's smirk said probably not. He smiled, a genuine one this time. Tad was always horny with him, which he found totally sexy and endearing.

"You have a one-track mind," he accused him, waving his fork at him.

Tad feigned shock, his hand at his throat like an old woman clutching her pearls. "Whatever do you mean? I have no idea what you're talking about!"

And then he spoiled the whole effect by winking at Zeke, who laughed out loud. Relaxing for the first time since Tad had shown up.

"You know exactly what I'm talking about, you fraud!" He grinned at Tad's fake outraged expression. "And I didn't know you were into that kind of kink."

Tad waggled his brows. "Everyone likes to think they're the boss of something."

Zeke's eyes went to Tad's lips, watching as his tongue peeked out to lick off the sauce from the lasagna. His heart rate ticked up. Growly, demanding Tad was fucking sexy, and just what he needed tonight.

"Maybe you can show me after dinner what you like to think you're the boss of, then." He raised a brow in what he hoped was a seductive manner and went back to his dinner.

Tad chuckled. "I don't think. I know."

Another eyebrow waggle accompanied that bit of boasting before they both collapsed into fits of laughter. They finished dinner, did the dishes and then Tad pulled him into the bathroom.

"Shower with me?" he asked. "One more time before I go."

Zeke spun him around so that they both faced the mirror. "Look at us," he ordered him. "Look at how good we look together."

He slid his hands down Tad's chest and settled them just inside the waistband of his dress pants. He could feel Tad's heart beginning to race and his breaths deepening.

"Touch me, babe!"

Tad's whispered plea set his senses reeling. He unbuttoned his fly and slid his fingers down to slip though the precum already leaking from the head of his dick. He smeared it around his cockhead, loving the way Tad leaned back against him and moaned. Zeke kissed the length of his lover's exposed neck, sucking a kiss bruise just where his neck met his shoulder.

"Oh, fuck, Zeke! Stop teasing me!"

"Why should I? I have to get my practice in before you leave me, don't I?" Shit! That had come out wrong!

Tad turned in his arms and cupped his face. "Leave you? I'm not leaving you, babe. I'll be back as soon as I can. I'll always come back to you."

Zeke nodded, all his uncertainty from earlier returning, and he knew when Tad figured it out.

"That's what's going on with you, isn't it? That's why you're so intense. You're worried about us, about me. About being so far away from each other."

224

Zeke couldn't lie. He needed Tad to make love to him, to remind him that he had nothing to worry about. But he was angry with himself and ashamed to admit he needed the reassurance. Tad didn't seem worried by the prospect of distance between them, so why was he such a fucking coward?

"Hey, look at me! Don't get lost in your head. I'm here. Let's talk about this."

Tad leaned his forehead against Zeke's, waiting for him. When he could speak without sounding like a lost child, he raised his head and looked Tad in the eyes as he spoke.

"I'm just not ready to be apart from you. I always knew your job could take you abroad, away from me. So yeah, I know this panicking is stupid, but that's the whole truth right there. This thing between us is so new, you know. And I've no experience with regular relationships, never mind long-distance ones."

Tad reached down between them and pressed his hand against the fly of Zeke's jeans. His cock, which was still plump from their earlier play, jerked. He pushed against Tad's hand, inviting more pressure, and Tad gave it to him.

"We're in this together, you and I. Everything you're feeling—the uncertainty, the fear—I'm feeling it as well. But this..." he squeezed Zeke's cock hard, "this is as real as it gets. And we're both feeling this, too, babe. I need you to be strong for me, like I'll be strong for you. We'll talk or message each other every day. We won't lose touch. And tonight, we'll touch each other all night, so we don't forget what it feels like to belong to each other. Okay? You with me?"

"Yeah."

That was all the whispered agreement of which Zeke was capable. Tad's voice, as much as his words, poured calm over Zeke's nerves, soothing them, easing the anxiety, leaving him ready to continue the seduction he had begun to help him forget how little time he had left before Tad was gone.

"Undress me!"

Tad's command stirred Zeke's blood. "You're not the boss of me," he said, recalling their dinner conversation and wanting to renew the play.

Tad growled and gripped his cock, squeezing it so hard it almost hurt before he released it and leaned in to say against Zeke's lips, "No. I'm more than just the boss of you. You're *mine*, and I get to tell you everything fucking thing I want to do to you, and you get to humor me because you want it, too. Am I fucking right, Nurse Taylor?" He stroked Zeke's now-rigid length while he waited for his reply.

"Sir, yes, sir!" Zeke dared to tease him in return.

"So, if you want my dick, you better fucking undress me. Now!"

Zeke couldn't tell anyone how he managed it, but Tad was naked in record time, and his own clothes apparently dissolved, since he had no recollection of having removed them. Then they were in the shower stall, standing beneath a fall of water, kissing and sucking each other off, rubbing their cocks together and roaring out their orgasms into each other's mouths. Finally spent, they rinsed off and went to bed, lying tangled in the sheets, drifting off to sleep in each other's arms.

Chapter Sixteen

October

The airport was crowded, but Tad saw Zeke as soon as he rounded the corner. He dragged his suitcase behind him, the garment bag draped over his shoulder adding to the weight of exhaustion he carried. But nothing could shake the joy he felt at the sight of the man he loved. It had been three long, very busy, extremely stressful weeks away, and he had never felt lonelier than he had this time. Not even in all his years in the service had he felt the devastating loss he felt being away from the man he knew he wanted by his side for the long haul. Logically, he knew the separations would ease in intensity as they grew to know each other better, and he couldn't wait for that time to come. But in the meantime, it was pure torture.

Zeke put his phone to his ear, and Tad felt his own buzz in his pocket. He didn't bother to try and answer; he was almost...there. He inhaled the unique scent of him deeply even as he called his lover's name.

"Zeke!"

Zeke turned and his eyes widened with relief and joy. "Hey!"

Tad leaned in and kissed him, not caring who saw or what they thought. "I've missed you, babe."

Zeke kissed him again, harder this time, and then pulled away. "Let's take this elsewhere. I have no desire to attract the attention of the public safety officers when I fuck your mouth with my tongue."

Tad laughed. "Who are you and what have you done with my boyfriend?"

Zeke's laughter was music in his ears. How had it come to this, that he was totally sold on a guy he hadn't known six months ago? He didn't know the answer, but he was grateful every day for the chance he'd finally been given to have his own person, someone meant just for him, and he was never letting go.

Zeke took the garment bag from him, and they walked out of the terminal hand in hand...another first for Tad, and one he found he liked a hell of a lot. The car was in the furthest parking lot, which was unsurprisingly almost totally deserted. Zeke barely let him put the suitcase and garment bag in the back before he was all over him. Tad reveled in the feel of his man in his arms as they kissed ravenously, Zeke making good on his promise to tongue-fuck his mouth.

"I missed you too, Popeye!"

One last soft kiss and then they got into the car. Zeke drove.

"Where are we headed?" he asked.

"Home." He heard the confusion in Zeke's answer.

"Mine or yours?"

Zeke glanced over at him, clearly puzzled by the question. Then he answered. "Whichever one you want to go to. It's your call."

Tad smiled. "Then let's go home to your place. I can drive myself to mine in the morning. If that's okay with you?"

He knew it was, but he wanted Zeke to reaffirm his decision to become a part of his life by letting him into his home. The last time they'd been together, the sex had been wildly fulfilling. This time, he wanted to go the tender route, to cement their growing commitment to each other. And he wanted to let Zeke know what his plans were for their future, if he would agree. Zeke reached over and took his hand, lacing their fingers together.

"I'm real glad you're back, Tad." He raised Tad's hand to his lips and kissed it.

"I'm glad to be back with you." This homecoming was better than the last one had been months ago, when he had dragged his exhausted ass home to his condo alone. The clients had signed the contract after putting a lot of obstacles in the way. Obstacles he had had to remove painstakingly, patiently, because the contract was that important...

"Oh shit! I remember!" The words burst from him as memories came flooding back. Memories of that missing month. "I remember!"

Zeke squeezed his hand. "Everything?"

He loved that Zeke didn't need to be brought up to speed. "Yes, everything." His joy dimmed a bit. "Everything."

"Tad? What is it, babe? What's wrong?"

"I remember why I was distracted at that red light." Sorrow welled up inside him as the full memory of that day emerged.

"Wanna talk about it?"

"Not now. When we get home, okay?" He needed time to process the memory and to grieve.

Zeke kept holding his hand while he tried to wrap his mind around what he had been hiding from himself. Ben was gone. He'd been on his way home from the office when he got the call. He had the green light and was moving off as he was being told his best friend had taken his own life when he heard the sound and looked up in time to see the truck heading directly for him. He remembered feeling dazed and panicked at the same time, not knowing what to do. And he remembered thinking *This is it. I'm gonna be with Ben soon.* Then nothing...until this moment.

Tears ran unheeded down his cheeks as he realized he had missed his friend's funeral. When Ben had needed him, Tad had not been there. What had happened to him? He had no one. He had been alone, except for Tad. And Tad had let him down in the end. Guilt and anger and sorrow raged inside him and he bit back the scream that welled up in his throat. He was grateful Zeke was there with him because he knew he wouldn't have been able to drive if he had remembered all this when he was on his own. He only hoped he'd be able to talk about it when they got home without blubbering like an idiot.

Thankfully, Zeke left him to his thoughts, and by the time they pulled up on his driveway, Tad was mostly back in control. He helped take his things inside and let Zeke fuss over him, taking the time to calm himself so he could share the memory that explained so much.

"What would you like to drink? Something hard or soft?"

Zeke was crouched in front of him, a look of concern in his brown eyes. "Soft, please. Maybe just some water, for now?" He didn't need alcohol messing with his thinking, even if a stiff drink sounded like a great idea.

"Okay. Here. Ready to talk now?"

Tad took the drink Zeke offered him and took a long swallow of water before setting it down. His hands were shaking and he didn't want to make a mess of the rug.

"Remember I told you about my friend Ben?"

"Yeah. What does he have to do with your memory coming back?"

Tad took a deep breath. "I was on my way home from the office when I got the call. They told me Ben had killed himself. They wanted me to know so I would send only enough money to bury him. And they wanted to know if I would be there at the funeral, or if I wanted to have any part in planning it. I was in shock, I guess. I hadn't answered them so we were still on the phone when I looked up. The light was green so I moved off and then saw the truck. I couldn't think what to do. I felt disoriented. And when I saw it heading for me, I thought I was gonna die and be with Ben."

He stopped to drink the rest of the water in the glass and then he added, "What if I could have avoided getting hurt? Maybe I could have made evasive maneuvers, you know? And what about Ben? When he needed me, in his last days, I wasn't there. And I wasn't even there to lay his body to rest. He had no one in the end...not even me."

This time the sorrow could not be banked. Tad felt strong arms wrap around him while he cried his eyes out. His soul was ablaze with grief and guilt, burning him up from the inside, and the tears only made the fire hotter. But he couldn't stop them, so he cried until he was spent. Zeke put him to bed, and the next morning, after making him drink a cup of coffee, he took him home. Tad didn't pay any attention to where they were going, and when he opened his eyes when the car stopped, he found himself outside the front door of his family home. Zeke had taken him home to his mother.

Love welled up inside him, right alongside the grief. Zeke could have kept him with him in his cute bungalow, but he knew Tad needed more than a new lover then, and he did what any good nurse would do...he gave him the best medicine for what ailed him. Fresh tears pooled behind his eyes, but he swallowed, refusing to let them fall. He was a grown man, not a boy. He could handle grief. And he could handle love. He got out of the car and took Zeke's hand, letting him lead him up the front steps.

When Bailey opened the door, the surprise on his face was tempered by a quiet joy when he saw their joined hands.

"Mr. Tad! Mr. Zeke! Good morning. What brings you home?"

"Good morning, Bailey. Tad has got his memory back, and I thought his mom should know. He needs her now."

Tad let Zeke speak for him, glad he was able to reprise his role as caregiver and do what needed to be done, because he seemed to have lost his mojo for the time being. Zeke led him up to his room while Bailey went to get his mother. By the time she got there, Tad was lying on the bed, shoes off, eyes closed. He heard Zeke speaking quietly to her and a door closed. He opened his eyes and saw his mother looking at him with mingled happiness and trepidation in her gaze. He didn't want to have to tell it again, but he knew he had to. And knowing his mother, she was going to insist he go for grief counseling. Maybe he wouldn't argue with her, since he was sure she'd be right, and he knew Zeke would agree with her.

The rest of the day and the day after were a blur. He didn't tell his mother about Ben until the next evening, after she had managed to coax him to eat some of the salad and soup Bailey made for him. This time, he told the story without tears, and for the first time that he could recall, his mother shed tears for someone other than her family.

"I'm so sorry, *mon chéri*. No one should be allowed to die alone, and no mother should desert her child. We will find out what happened to Ben, and anything you wish to do for him now will be wonderful, from one friend to another."

Zeke called him that night, and Tad invited him over for dinner the next day. He knew it was time to tell his mother about them, though he suspected she might already have a fair idea on her own.

"I'll send the car for you," he told his lover. "Five okay?"

"Sure, five is fine. But only if you're sure. I don't want you stressing yourself…"

"Zeke, stop. I'm okay, I promise. Still hurting, but we both know that will ease in its own good time. I'll deal."

"I know you will. You're much braver than you think."

The words warmed his heart. He needed to feel worthy of this man's love. And he needed to tell him how he felt.

"See you tomorrow, then. Sleep sweet, babe."

Nothing could dispel the case of nerves that made him sleep poorly. Neither yoga nor swimming nor lifting helped. By the time Zeke arrived, looking sexier than ever in thigh-hugging black jeans and a white Polo shirt stretched deliciously over his broad chest, Tad was as tightly wound as a corkscrew. And Zeke, being the observant man he was, noticed at once.

"Hey, what's up? You're so tense!" He gave Tad a long, warm hug before letting him go.

"I'm just stressing all the things I need to say to you and to my mother. I'll be fine, once it's over."

He saw the look that came and went on Zeke's face and could smack himself. That hadn't been the best way to explain his tension. He tried again.

"It's not bad news, I promise. But this whole memory return has me thinking I need to stop putting off the things I need to say to the people who matter to me. And that includes you. Okay? Nothing bad is gonna happen."

Dinner, surprisingly enough, was the most relaxed it had ever been with his mother at the table. She asked after Zeke's grandmother and seemed genuinely delighted Mrs. Taylor had chosen to stay in the home.

"She can be independent and still be looked after in an emergency. And how lovely she can keep her pet. What's his name again?"

"Punkin," Zeke said with a chuckle. "He's a pug."

His mother chuckled. "We used to have dogs," she said, and Tad didn't miss the wistful note in her voice. "But after Tad's father passed, I just couldn't…" She looked away for a moment, lost in thought, and then she took a deep breath and finished her thought. "I didn't have the wherewithal to be a good pet parent. So, I gave them up for adoption."

"Maybe it's time to change that, *Maman*." it was time for a change all around, and Tad was ready to begin. "It seems like it's something you're willing to think about again."

She smiled. "Perhaps you're right, Tad." Then she turned her eyes to Zeke. "And have you found a new job, Mr. Taylor?"

Before he knew it, dinner was over, and they were in the sitting room sipping after-dinner drinks when Tad decided it was time.

"I wanted to speak to the two of you together," he began, "and this seems as good a time as any to do it."

Zeke remained silent, predictably, but his mother spoke the question he had no doubt Zeke also had on his mind.

"What is it, *mon chéri*?"

"Ben's death has really shaken me up. I don't know if I'll ever get over it. But I do know I can't go on being the same guy I was. That's not enough for me anymore. Life's too short to waste time. I could have lost mine, but I didn't because, as Zeke believes, everything happens for a reason."

He turned to face his mother to say the next words. "*Maman*, I'm in a relationship with Zeke. I know you'd have preferred it be a woman, and I'm sorry if you're disappointed, but I've made my decision. Zeke is it for me. That's all I'm ready to say for now, but I wanted you to know."

There was so much more he wanted to say, but he couldn't until he had told Zeke how he felt and they had talked about their future. He waited for his mother to respond, wondering if the affable woman from dinner would remain or disappear under the weight of her disapproval. He didn't care either way.

"I'm happy for you, my son," she said at last. "I would never stand in your way. I hope you know that."

She stood up then, and walked over to where he sat. Leaning in, she kissed his cheek. "I'll leave the two of you alone now." She turned to Zeke and smiled. "Thank you for bringing my son home to me, Mr. Taylor. You are a kind and understanding man. I appreciate you."

Tad chuckled at the disbelief on Zeke's face as he watched his mother walk out of the room.

"What just happened here?" he asked, dumbfounded.

"I believe it's called gratitude and being grown up. My mother can be an adult when she wishes to be. And she knows when she's been given a second chance to do better. Trust me when I say, she is very grateful to you."

He shrugged. "I only did what was right."

He said it like it was the most obvious position to take. Tad shook his head incredulously. Zeke had no idea what a treasure he was. His humility was inspiring.

"So, you said you had things to say to both of us. I'm dying to hear what you have to say to me. And I want to know if you have any ideas about why you're still here instead of with Ben. What's the reason?"

Tad smiled. Another thing he loved about Zeke was how direct he was. No beating around the bush, just straight to the point. A man would always know where he stood with him.

"I think I was spared so I could know what it was to belong to someone, and to have someone be mine. I was spared so I could know love."

He stood up, suddenly more serious than he had ever been about anything in his whole life. None of the accolades he'd won for his work in the Navy, nor the contracts he had fought for and won since he began work in his father's company, meant as much as this moment with the man he loved. Being able to tell Zeke how he felt was overwhelming and special. He pulled Zeke to his feet and held his hands.

"I need you to know I'm in love with you, Aaron Melchizedek Taylor. And I want a future with you in it. I'd like to make my mother happy by giving her grandchildren, and I'm willing to do it in any way you prefer. But I can't do any of this alone. I need you to agree with me. So, this is the plan I came up with. We date each other for about another eight months or so, and while we're dating, we plan the picture perfect wedding. We get engaged, then get married and have some babies. You move in with me, or I move in with you, or we get something new that we both choose together. You introduce your Gram to my mom. We make a new family."

He stopped speaking and examined his lover's face, looking for any sign of his thoughts. Zeke kept his expression neutral, and Tad sighed in resignation.

He had gotten this far. He would say the rest and then leave it up to fate.

"So, what do you say, babe? Do you think this is a good plan?"

Zeke held his gaze for a moment longer and then leaned in to whisper, "I need a more private setting to give you my answer. Can you think of any place where we can be properly alone, Popeye?"

Tad saw the gleam in his eye and smiled. "I have just the place. If you promise to make it worth my while."

Zeke struck then, pulling him in for a devouring kiss that left him completely breathless and turned on beyond belief. Guess he'd take that as a promise.

Before long, they lay naked and tangled together on Tad's balcony, their heavy breathing punctuating the moans and sighs they uttered as they worked each other over. Zeke's tongue caressed Tad's cock in slow swirls inside his mouth, while Tad opened his throat and swallowed around Zeke's dick. The groan of pleasure thrummed around Tad's cock, sending his temperature higher. Zeke sucked him harder, then released his length, keeping only the head in his mouth and suckling it like a baby.

"Fuck! You're gonna make me cum, babe."

Incoherent gurgling was his only response as Zeke swallowed him down to the root again. He dove back in, determined to pay Zeke back with the same level of pleasure as he was receiving. Zeke withdrew again, jacking him off while he licked the head, teasing and tormenting him. He sucked on his finger and drew it through the precum leaking from his lover's dick before pushing it into his hole. Zeke gasped, releasing his cock to catch a breath at the unexpected intrusion. Tad knew how much he loved being finger-fucked, and he worked his way in until he could slide against his prostate.

Zeke muffled his scream of pleasure by stuffing Tad's dick back into his mouth and sucking hard. Tad gasped in reaction and fucked Zeke's mouth, urging his lover to do the same to him. Finally, knowing how he wanted the night to end, Tad pulled away from Zeke and tapped his thigh.

"Come here," he said, his voice hoarse from deep-throating Zeke's cock.

Zeke repositioned himself and Tad drew him in for a dirty kiss, all tongues and teeth. And then he made his request.

"I need you to do me a solid, Zeke," he began, slowing the kiss, turning it tender and seductive.

"Oh, yeah? And what might that be?"

Tad inhaled deeply. "I need you to fuck me, babe!"

He caught Zeke's startled inhale in another kiss and pressed their cocks together, sliding his own over Zeke's, moaning with how good it felt.

"Are you serious?"

"As a JAG," Tad replied with a smirk. "You have a problem with that?"

Maybe he was moving too fast. Or maybe Zeke didn't want to top. Tad didn't care which he did, but he didn't want to force something on his lover that would make him uncomfortable.

"No...but you know you'll have to help me get it right, right?"

Zeke sounded so nervous. It was adorable and sexy how this big, tough nurturer still needed someone like Tad to help him see his worth.

"Well, for starters, you need to relax. Think about how good it feels when I fuck you. Think about what you like when I do it. I can promise you, everything you like me to do, I'll like you to do."

While he spoke, he reached over for the lube and condom he had pulled from his drawer before leading Zeke outside. Opening the tube of lube, he handed it to Zeke and said, "Start by opening and lubing me up so I can be ready for your cock. You know how you love when I finger you, babe?"

"Yeah. It's so fucking good, every single time."

Tad smiled. "That's because of that magical button called your prostate. It's the male love button, and if you find it, you'll make me see stars, guaranteed."

He stole another kiss and watched as Zeke lubed up his fingers and slathered some around his hole. The touch ignited him in a way he hadn't been by anyone in a very long time. Zeke's hand was big, his fingers long and thick. He seemed to be concentrating, and Tad felt him circle his hole before pushing in. He relaxed and watched as Zeke felt the warmth of his body around his single digit.

"Oh, holy fuck! You're tight!" He turned anxious eyes to Tad's face. "Is this okay, do you like it??"

"It's fine, babe. Push all the way in. Yes, just like that." He felt his body relax the more Zeke pushed into him. "Ah!" He hissed as Zeke's finger brushed against his prostate. "Do that again!"

Zeke nailed him again and he groaned. "Oh, baby! Give it to me. I need another one, love."

Zeke sank a second finger inside him and started to fuck him in earnest. Tad rocked his hips to catch every inch of the two fingers shuttling in and out of him.

"One more, baby. Give me one more, please!"

"You're so fucking hot when you beg me, Tad!"

Zeke's breath was hitching as he lubed up a third finger and slid it inside Tad's hole. Tad rocked back against him, hungry for the touches that would drive him closer to the edge. When Zeke nailed his prostate again in a renewed three-pronged assault, he roared and fought to keep his body under enough control so he wouldn't cum.

"Baby, it's time. I need your cock in me. Now!"

He didn't wait for Zeke to react. He couldn't, he was that desperate to feel him inside. He reached for the condom and ripped the packet open, sliding the protection over Zeke's girth and then dumping lube all over it. By the time he was done, his hands were trembling. He slid a finger in with Zeke's three and growled when together they hit his gland again.

"Oh, fuuuuuck! Now, baby, please, fuck me now!"

He was babbling like a baby, needy and horny and hard as stone. Zeke lined up his cock and pushed in, so slowly it was the most excruciatingly pleasurable torture Tad had ever endured. He couldn't wait any longer. He was going to spill before Zeke ever got a stroke in if he didn't get inside him right fucking now. He raised his legs and thrust up, ignoring the burn as Zeke's cock pierced his hole and he bottomed out inside.

Zeke didn't move. He waited, no doubt to get his own body under enough control so he would last long enough to get Tad off.

"Oh, shit, this is worse torture than what you do to me, babe. I don't wanna move for fear I blow, but God, it's so hard when all I wanna do is ram the fuck outta your tight ass."

The dirty talk was making things worse, but Tad loved how pleasure was unravelling Zeke.

"Ram me, Zeke. Fucking ram me! Do it!"

He reached back and pulled on Zeke's hips over and over until he started fucking him in earnest. Their hips slapped together, flesh against flesh. Zeke's growl began low in his throat, and the harder he drove into Tad, the louder it became.

"Yes, baby, take me just like that!"

Tad slammed his hips up to meet Zeke's downward press and they fucked wildly. Neither of them was gonna last long this first time, but he didn't care. It was so damned good. And when Zeke changed his body's angle, his dick rode over his prostate. Tad lost control, screaming into Zeke's neck as he shot cum over their abs and chests. He couldn't slow down, and he squeezed Zeke's dick in his ass, wanting him to blow as well.

"Cum for me, Zeke! Cum hard, baby! Cum now!"

Zeke blew, losing control of his strokes, slamming into Tad until he froze and wailed.

"Taaaaaaad! Jesus!"

They fell back, Zeke sprawled on top of Tad, both of them fighting for breath. Zeke was heavy, but Tad didn't care. He needed his lover's weight to ground him, to keep him earthbound while he processed his emotions. He needed him close.

Zeke rolled to the side and pulled Tad with him, uncaring of the semen between their sweaty bodies.

"I love you, too, Thaddeus Meredith, III. And yes, I like your plan. It's a real good plan. Just one thing." He leaned in and nipped Tad's bottom lip.

"What's that, babe?"

"I want a real proposal." He licked the place he'd just nipped, and then sank his tongue into Tad's mouth.

When Zeke let him up for air, Tad laughed. He could manage that.

CPSIA information can be obtained
at www.ICGtesting.com
Printed in the USA
LVHW082320270819
629196LV00027B/887/P

9 781080 737437